A Beautiful Surprise

ROBBI RENEE

#BLP

B. Love Publications

Visit bit.ly/readBLP to join our mailing list for sneak peeks and release day links!

B. Love Publications - where Authors celebrate black men, black women, and black love.

To submit a manuscript for consideration, email your first three chapters to blovepublications@gmail.com with SUBMISSION as the subject.

The BLP Podcast – bit.ly/BLPUncovered

Let's connect on social media!
    Facebook - B. Love Publications
    Twitter - @blovepub
    Instagram - @blovepublications

Synopsis

Kismet or Karma?

    Fate or Far-fetched?

    Love or Lust?

    Friend or Foe?

Jameson Davenport's sexy swag is undeniable in Haven Pointe. The youngest son of the Davenport family dynasty, Jameson is not a man who promises any woman tomorrow. What you see is what you get. And what the ladies get from Jameson is an unforgettable night of fiery, thigh-aching passion. But what happens when his playboy behaviors are no longer fulfilling?

Giselle Dean, owner of Bonafide Beauty Boutique, is a pretty, curvaceous beauty, and wellness extraordinaire who's more than ready to ring wedding bells with her fiancé. However, love plays unsuspecting tricks on her when she finds herself massaging more than her best friend's injuries, causing her to reflect on what she really wants... or who.

Jameson and Giselle find themselves in unfamiliar territory. However, it's one filled with unexpected pleasantries and revitalizing passion. What happens when best friends collide? Is it a beautiful surprise or a hideous catastrophe? Check out Jameson and Giselle and see how they tow the line of becoming lovers and friends.

My sixth book! Who knew that when I wrote my first novella, 'French Kiss Christmas', that almost two years later, I would have six books under my belt?

This book is dedicated to Stephanie Nicole Norris. Without her author challenge on Facebook, I would not have stepped into this Robbi Renee journey. Thank you!

And to Diem Diamonds, Wesleigh's Besties, and all of the book reviewers, bloggers, beta readers, and fans, I thank you from the bottom of my heart.

One

"JD, WHAT ARE YOU DOING HERE?" I sighed, ambling into my townhouse. I spotted my friend Jameson Davenport's all-black Land Rover parked in front of my house. Giving him a key was clearly a mistake. It was strictly for emergencies, but clearly, his ass couldn't follow directions. Dropping my keys in the basket on the sofa table, I irritably eyed him lazing comfortably on my plush couch.

"I would be happy to trade this townhouse for that beautiful loft you rarely occupy." I rolled my eyes because this dude was way too cozy on my new royal blue couch.

"Man, don't start that shit. I told you, you can have that loft. I need sleep, Gilly. And you know you're the only one who can help me." Jameson grimaced as he repositioned on the couch.

"Really? At almost one o'clock in the morning on a Saturday night." I lazily sauntered into the kitchen to grab a bottle of water before returning to the living room. "Where is your nasty ass coming from anyway, JD? What girl's heart did you break tonight?"

Jameson slowly sat up, glaring at me with a devilish smile on his face.

"It's actually Sunday morning and I—" He abruptly halted. That cute smile quickly transformed into a scowl when he noticed the redness dimming my eyes.

"Yo, who the fuck I gotta see about these tears, man?" Jameson practically growled.

I rubbed my eyes, vainly attempting to erase any traces of sorrow.

"Nobody. It's nothing, JD. I don't want to talk about it."

"Is it nothing, or you don't want to talk about it? Which one, Gilly?" Jameson was a bully and never accepted no for an answer. He quickly diminished the space between us.

"I don't want to talk about it." I aggressively wiped the traitorous tear that escaped my tired orbs.

Moving quickly to avoid his interrogation, I darted up the steps toward my bedroom while shouting, "Get on the massage table! I'll be there in a minute!"

Jameson briskly followed, gently clutching my arm, halting my pursuit toward the bedroom. Turning my body to face him, he muttered, "Nah, man, stop playing. What happened, Giselle?"

I deeply inhaled before audibly and dramatically exhaling through puffed cheeks. Jameson ushered me into the bedroom, settling on the footboard bench while I timidly balled up, leaning against the linen-colored tufted headboard. Jameson glared at me, repeatedly, roughly rubbing his knuckles together. He was ready to fuck shit up once I disclosed my reason for the tears. Head buried in the pillow, I tapped my tongue against my teeth as I often did when nervous.

"Aye. Stop playing. Eyes on me." He moved to join me against the headboard, firmly nudging my chin and forcing a connection.

"And stop making that damn noise with your tongue. That shit is just weird."

"Shut up, JD." I paused, no conversation. Voiceless.

"Nigga! My damn shoulder is hurting. Tell me what the hell happened so you can fix this shit. I'm sleepy," he barked.

I cuddled against the pillow tighter and divulged one of the most embarrassing and heartbreaking nights of my life.

Five Hours Earlier

"GG, maybe this is a bad idea. We should go back to my house and think this through." My best friend and sister-in-law, Kayla, pleaded as I slowly crept down Hamilton Avenue in Kayla's brand-new white Tesla. My truck's gaslight was on, so I practically stole Kay's car and forced her to join me on this manhunt. I leaned my head out of the open window, circling the unfamiliar neighborhood in the heart of the city about twenty minutes from my home in Haven Pointe.

"Really, Kay? Your ass was hyping me up an hour ago. You were real quick to show me the IG screenshot, but now you wanna think about this shit. Fuck that." I picked up my cell phone and pressed a button on the screen and yelled, "Call Ahmad!"

This was at least the tenth time that I called my fiancé, Ahmad Holton, with no answer. Kayla connected her hands in prayer as her lips rapidly moved in silence. Shit, I bowed my head in prayer too. I prayed that he would pick up the phone. That what I knew in my heart to be true was just an ugly dream. I prayed we would get out of this neighborhood unscathed and more importantly, that I wouldn't commit homicide.

"GG, I was wrong. This is stupid. We are too grown for this." Kayla repositioned in the front seat to face me. "Ok, so

3

you find him… and then what? You gonna fight the girl? Fight him?"

I didn't answer. My doe-like chestnut eyes were wide and wet with tears. Kayla followed my line of sight. "Oh shit," she mumbled.

A familiar customized, charcoal gray Hummer H2 was parked on the street in front of a row of old, somewhat dilapidated brick houses. It was Ahmad's. He bought it as a present to himself when he opened his third Mosaic Art Bar in 2019. Anyone who knew Ahmad would notice his truck from ten miles away, with the custom paint, rims, and blackened windows tinted darker than what was probably legal.

Slowly pulling up behind his truck, I contemplated my next move. I gripped the steering wheel so tight, blisters started to form on my palms. Hot tears salted the corners of my mouth.

"GG," Kayla whispered, placing a hand on my shoulder. "Don't."

"Did she tell you which house, Kay?" I sharply turned my head, nostrils flared, fiery orbs burning holes through her face. "You can stay in the car. I don't care. This ends tonight."

Kayla frantically typed on her phone but remained hushed.

"Kay! What the fuck? What's the address?"

Shrugging her shoulders, Kayla remained silent while still hectically navigating her phone.

Since she didn't respond to my inquiry fast enough, I was ready to take matters into my own hands.

"Fuck it! I will knock on every goddamn door until I find his ass."

I aggressively reached to unlatch the seat belt but couldn't find the button because everything was fancy in this damn car.

"He clearly doesn't give a fuck about me. His ass ain't trying to hide when he parks a one-hundred-thousand-dollar customized truck with personalized plates in the damn ghetto. This bitch's pussy must be made of gold!" I continued my frenzied rant while still wrestling with the seat belt.

"Oh my God! Get a regular fucking car why don't you!" I yelled at Kayla, but she allowed me to self-destruct.

Resting my forehead on the steering wheel, I completely broke down. The vehement tears wouldn't cease. The distress, fear, and rage boiled into an uncontrollable inferno. Now I could completely understand how random women named Mary Jo living in poor-ville Georgia murdered their husbands with antifreeze-laced Gatorade. They simply *snapped*!

Wrath couldn't describe the madness I experienced. My skin was hot to the touch as if I was feverish, my right foot erratically tapped on the floor of the car, and a balled fist pounded the steering wheel. The new car smell was becoming increasingly irritating as my lividity and unease climaxed. I could see my episode of *Snapped*.

Giselle Lorena Dean, thirty-two, charged with homicide after lighting up the whole block on Hamilton Avenue in search of her cheating ass fiancé.

Blankly staring at the license plate on Ahmad's truck, I eyed the letters M-O-S-A-I-C, unconsciously fondling the stunning three-carat platinum set engagement ring.

"GG. Let's just go. We can get a few bottles of wine and devise a plan," Kayla recommended.

"A plan? The plan was to catch him cheating and beat his fucking ass!" I shouted.

"Beat his ass? Really? Ahmad is what—six three, two hundred and forty pounds? Which one of us was beating his ass?" Kayla motioned her coffin-shaped nail between us.

She was about six inches over five feet and maybe 180 pounds soaking wet. I, on the other hand, was what Meghan termed *a stallion*. Five feet, nine inches, and an easy 215 pounds. I thought I could give it a valiant effort—at least land a few good punches to that perfectly chiseled sun-kissed yellow face of his.

"You wanna confirm what you already know?" Kayla continued, disrupting the slight smile on my face at the thought of punching Ahmad. "You need to see it to believe it? Because that nigga has left enough receipts all up and through the city, boo."

I sighed because Kayla was right. Since proposing a year ago, Ahmad had been different... distant. The foundational friendship and normal loving banter were fading. And while sex with Ahmad was always good as hell because that man was slanging a log, it seemed more out of necessity than desire, lacking the sensuality and intimacy that once rendered me weak. And let's not forget the countless pictures of him on social media with random women in his clubs. He always said that it came with the territory of being a bar owner, but I wasn't convinced.

The post that sparked this moronic mad dash across town to do God only knows what, was a picture of a half-naked Ahmad on a beach in the Dominican Republic with a woman whose IG name was *QueenofdaLou*. The caption read, *I don't want my time to end in paradise or with him.* Eagle spread wings with the name *Micki* inscribed inside of a heart was tattooed across the back of the faceless man in the picture. The expanse of his back couldn't be denied because I was intimate with every muscle and cord—every intricate detail of that tattoo. *Micki.* Ahmad's mother, Michelle Holten, lost her battle with breast cancer six months ago, and he got the tattoo shortly before she died.

At the time of the picture, Ahmad was supposed to be in New York visiting his father, but clearly, he was gallivanting with some barely clothed no-name bitch on the beach. According to his text message earlier this morning, his flight was arriving back in St. Louis at eight o'clock tonight. Kayla's inspector gadget friend also informed us that the no-named chick lived on Hamilton Avenue in north St. Louis city but didn't know the address.

It was clear to me Ahmad gave zero fucks at this point. His tattooed, sexy ass body sprawled over Instagram and the customized truck that everybody in the city recognized as his parked in front of a random house was a clear indication of the *I don't give a fuckness* he possessed.

"This nigga straight up on some hoe shit." I shook my head, recollecting the moment he bought the truck.

"Nah, he's on some bald-headed hoe shit!" Kayla screeched.

"I just want to fuck his shit up. I want to make him hurt like I am right now. I can't breathe, Kay. Why would he do this? I've always told him to just walk away from this relationship the moment I was no longer enough. Ugh!" I released a gut-wrenching cry. Kayla reached across the car, pulling me into a firm hug.

"You don't want to do this, GG. This is not you, boo. You have just as much to lose as he does. Ahmad's ain't shit ass ain't worth it. I bet that musty bitch ain't got shit on you, with her busted ass weave." Kayla scowled before we both released a disorderly guffaw.

Once again, my best friend for the win. I did have a lot to lose. Not only my dignity but my brand and reputation in this city. As the owner of Bonafide Beauty Boutique and a certified esthetician, makeup artist, and massage therapist, I had a growing business to manage.

Ahmad and I were rising stars in the city. We'd both received the St. Louis Forty under Forty Award and were featured on the cover of the *Black Business Magazine* as a Power One Hundred couple. So, the fact that Ahmad was callously out in these streets was mind-blowing and fucking disrespectful.

"You're right. Let's get the hell out of here." I reached for a key to start the car but forgot I was in Kayla's fancy ass Tesla. I pressed the pedal to restart the car, but it would not budge. "Kay, did you charge this thing?" I fussed.

"Yes. It has a full charge." Kayla pointed to the green indicator light. "It was just delivered yesterday. Your ass has driven it more than me. Try it again."

I attempted again and nothing. "Do you have to do something special? It started just fine at your house."

Kayla scrambled to find the owner's manual while I searched for instructions on Google.

"Hey Siri, how do you start a Tesla?" I blurted.

"I am not sure I understand your question. You can purchase a Tesla at www.tesla.com. Should I take you there now?" Siri irritably questioned.

"Whenever I meet that bitch Siri, I'm whupping her ass." I confirmed it to nobody but myself. "This is ridiculous. If this was a gas-guzzling, regular old car, we wouldn't be dealing with this shit," I fussed.

"For your information, bitch, I am saving the planet. And have you seen these gas prices lately? No thanks, hunty." Kayla sarcastically smirked before frantically flipping through the manual. "Shit! How many languages come before English?"

My brown eyes connected with her light hazel orbs as a boisterous laugh escaped our lungs. It was always an adventure when the two of us collided. That laugh felt good though. I needed a little comic relief in the midst of my shitty life right now.

"Ok, I got it. Press and hold the brake, and it should start within ten seconds," Kayla instructed.

"Yo, Ahmad. Get at me when you are ready for a new DJ at your spot, dawg. I got my shit together for real this time." An unfamiliar male voice echoed in the night air.

"Meech, you still talking shit?" A mellow-tone female voice laughed.

The rapid rise and fall of my chest was sporadic. *Am I having a heart attack? I think I'm having a heart attack.* The thought of Ahmad cheating was one thing, but the reality of seeing it live and in living color was downright dreadful. I glanced in the rearview mirror, checking my face as if how I appeared mattered. *Dummy.* The shit was about to hit the fan; fucked up hair, no earrings, and fresh face be damned.

"Drive, GG!" Kayla whispered, anxiously gritting through her pearly white teeth.

Ahmad's familiar imposing frame stood on the patio at 180 Hamilton Avenue, and he wasn't alone. I was frozen. The sight of Ahmad lovingly embracing this woman, a fucking beautiful woman at that, snatched every iota of my peace and sanity. This chick looked properly fucked and happily satisfied —by my goddamn man. And dammit, her weave was perfect. At least a busted sew-in would've given me a little reprieve. The woman whispered against his ear, and he heartily laughed. Like snickered loudly. This mutherfucker had been properly fucked too.

"Give me a few days. I'll hit you." Ahmad kissed her cheek. "Now get your ass in the house." Patting her butt, he was playful with her. Like he literally palmed her manufactured ass. Ahmad turned to walk down the crumbled steps of no-name's old ass house, simultaneously pulling his phone from the back pocket of his jeans.

My phone's blare sounded like a sonic boom, jolting me from what felt like a momentary stroke. I immediately pulled from the parking space, making a U-turn to head back to where I came from.

"Don't answer it. He probably saw us," Kayla nervously mumbled.

I shook my head, confident that Ahmad didn't see us, especially since he was unfamiliar with Kayla's new car.

"Hello," I groggily answered.

"GG, you sleep, baby?" Ahmad's timbre sounded just as loving and free as it did with the no-name woman.

"Just about," I emotionlessly whispered.

"I'm on my way home. My flight was delayed. You need anything?" Ahmad lied.

"No. I'm at my house anyway."

Jesus had to be driving the car because I couldn't see a damn thing through the tsunami in my eyes.

"Oh. You didn't tell me that you weren't at my house." He sounded disappointed. Would he have stayed at no-name's house?

"We haven't talked, Ahmad. How was your trip? How's Mr. Holton?" I probed. My demeanor was eerily calm.

"You know Pops. He's chillin'." This mutherfucker was smoothly lying. No flinch, no pause.

The chuckle I released was more like an uncomfortable grunt. The effortless nature of his ability to lie was astonishing —disturbing. I had to pull the car over before I killed me and Kayla or whipped this damn Tesla around to go back and kill Ahmad. Kayla's orbs were a mile wide, anticipating my next move.

"Get some sleep, babygirl." Ahmad's tone was laced with what I once would've labeled love.

I nodded, unable to formulate words. "Okay," hushly leaked from my lips.

"Aye. I missed you," Ahmad whispered, then ended the call.

Jameson's eyebrows collided as he intently listened to my story. He leered at me with narrowed eyes for a long, uneasy minute.

"Gilly, are you fucking kidding me? You went on H-Ave in

a damn Tesla with Kayla's scary ass? You coulda got your ass shot over there just so them hood niggas could take that car for a joy ride!" Jameson yelled.

"Really, J! I'm being scolded for going to the hood? Is that all you got out of that whole story?" I angrily threw the pillow at his head.

"Nah. I got everything I needed to get out of that dumbass story. He's cheating. Ok? So, what are you gonna do about it? Sit your ass here and cry with me? Ain't shit I can do. What if that nigga would've laid hands on you? Then I would've had to lay hands on his bitch ass. You know I'll do that for you, but then what?" He paused, lifting his brow, searching my face for an answer. "Huh, Gil? Then what?"

"I don't know," I mutedly whimpered.

"Nah. Say that shit from your chest because your ass was big and bad when you drove down on the ave." He aggressively flicked my chin. Jameson was pissed. "Then what?"

"I don't know!" I yelled. "He's breaking my fucking heart, JD. Things have been rocky for a minute, but that doesn't change the way this makes me feel. I just want him to hurt like I'm hurting. I want him to know how it feels to see the person he loves with somebody else. Loving and kissing somebody else. Being loved by somebody else."

Jameson shook his head, seemingly in disgust, but he scooted closer to me anyway, allowing me to weep in his lap.

Leaning down to kiss the side of my temple, he whispered, "So do something about it, Giselle."

Two

"NAH, I'm busting that nigga's head on sight," my brother, Jericho, proclaimed as he slammed his gun holster on the kitchen counter. I came over for breakfast just like I did every Sunday morning.

"And Kayla Dean, what the hell were you thinking hyping her up, knowing GG's ass will fight anybody?" he said to his wife and my best friend since the third grade. "You know she thinks she's Laiya Ali and shit."

Last night, when I thought Kayla was texting her cousin to get the no-name woman's real name and exact address, she was texting Jericho, confessing about our little road trip. He was prepared to intercept, but thankfully, that wasn't necessary. Jericho was a police captain in St. Louis County and was often ready to fuck up shit over his baby sister.

"I'm sorry, baby. We were both so pissed and a little tipsy, so..." Kayla's voice trailed off once Jericho clutched her ass, pulling her into his frame.

"Real talk, that shit could've ended bad. I don't want to have to kill a nigga over my two favorite girls." Jericho winked at me and kissed Kayla.

He closed the distance between us and lifted my chin with his finger, commanding, "You're better than that shit, G."

I nodded.

"Don't tell Mommy and Daddy, ok? I'll talk to them when I'm ready," I pleaded. Our father, Jericho Sr., would join his son in the crusade to bust Ahmad in the head.

"What do you know for sure?" Jericho lifted his brow in question. My mother, Lorena Dean, would ask us that question when we behaved out of character.

Biting my cheek couldn't quell the mist in my eyes or the quiver against my lips. My big brother lifted my head, his eyes restating the question with no words.

"I know my worth. I know who and whose I am. I am beautifully and wonderfully made," I whispered.

"That's right. You ain't lost shit. Ahmad will be on the losing end of this one, babygirl."

"You sound like Jameson. He said the same thing," I chirped, drying my eyes so I could finish devouring the seafood quiche Kayla cooked.

"When did you see Jameson? I thought you went home last night," Kayla inquired, moving throughout the kitchen to fix Jericho a plate.

"I did. But you know JD. The emergency key is used for whatever he defines as an emergency. He was at my house when I got there last night." I rolled my eyes, mulling over Jameson's fussing last night.

I didn't need to check the guest room this morning to know that Jameson was gone. He often rose before the sun to workout with his trainer. Pain or lack of sleep never halted his routine.

After he all but forced me to stop crying, I gave him a thirty-minute hot stone massage and acupuncture therapy. JD was snoring on the massage table I had in the loft maybe fifteen minutes into the session. I gently nudged him awake, encouraging him to transition to the queen-size bed in the guest room.

While Jameson was sound asleep, slumber eluded me. I cycled through bouts of angst, sadness, rage, and then endless tears. The sudden illumination of the room from the glare on my phone scared me.

"Yeah, JD," I answered.

"Stop all that fucking crying, man. Do you need me to come in there?" Jameson's groggy bass-filled tenor was vexed.

"No," I whined, secretly wishing I could cry in his arms again, shit, somebody's arms. But Jameson's drill sergeant ass never thought crying was appropriate. He was about solutions.

"Man, there's no crying in baseball, and there's no crying in life. Gilly, take your ass to sleep. You are better than this. You're a boss, baby. You're going to be fine."

"I know, but just give me this one night. Please. I'll rekindle my boss bitch behavior tomorrow."

"Shoulder pain again?" Kayla's probing rocked me back into the present.

"Yep."

"Maybe if he decreases the number of hoes he's running through, he wouldn't be in so much pain." We all laughed.

Jameson was definitely a ladies' man. Young, old, fat, skinny, rich, or poor, the ladies *loved* cool J. But what was there not to love?

Jameson was a six-foot, athletic-framed, coffee-hued god. Deep hazel eyes magnificently contrasted against his dark unblemished skin. Perfectly tapered coils, thick ample lips, and a python-length tongue that could not go unnoticed. He was Michael B. Jordan and Adonis Creed wrapped in one delicious package.

The beauty shop gossip also revealed that he was nasty as fuck in the bedroom. *'No limit soldier'* was his nickname amongst the ladies. As his friend, I often witnessed the outrageous behavior of dickmatized women who fell victim to Jameson's charm. My favorite was Fatima. This dumb girl took the time to write various personalized *I hate you* messages on a brick before throwing it through the windshield of his Land Rover.

Charming was truly the best way to describe him. Jameson was just so carefree, jovial, and spontaneous that it was difficult to be anything but happy in his presence. Jameson was like a plague you willingly desired to contract. Handsomely contagious.

"I don't think JD is slowing down any time soon." Jericho chortled. "Young Bull got smarts, money, and got his shit together, so bitches, I mean women are going to be on his dick, I mean jock," he corrected after Kayla tossed a flaming glare across the kitchen.

Tossing my head back, I hollered, laughing at the control Kayla had over my brother. My eyes misted as Jericho quickly diminished their separation, drawing her into a loving embrace.

I envied their love. Shit, their closeness and friendship were coveted. According to my brother, he'd been in love with Kayla since we were in the third grade while he was in the fifth. After years of innocent adolescent flirting, they officially started dating in high school and never parted. They were each other's first... everything.

Even when Jericho joined the Air Force and was gone for four years, they both remained faithful. As soon as he returned home to complete his degree, he immediately proposed to a twenty-year-old Kayla, and they'd been happily married for ten years.

I wasn't so lucky in love like Jericho. I had countless boyfriends in high school and college. A few serious relationships and a few sex buddies. Also, unlike my brother, I was sexually exploratory, always seeking the next best dick.

And then I met Ahmad Deon Holten. My Lord. That man had me screaming for mercy while begging him for more in the same damn breath. We met at a masquerade party hosted by the National Panhellenic Council to raise funds for historically black colleges and universities. Ahmad was new to the city with plans to open a bar that combined his love for art and bourbon. Dressed in a charcoal gray suit, crisp white shirt, a purple and gold tie, and mask donning his fraternity colors, he wasn't coy in expressing his attraction to me. His Herculean physique crowded every thread of that damn suit. Steph Curry in the face but built like a damn defensive lineman, Ahmad was fine, like fine, fine. After sensually frolicking on the dance floor all night and inhaling too many old-fashioned bourbons, I giddily accepted his offer for a nightcap in his hotel room. That man sucked and slurped my pussy so good, I swear my ass sang a negro spiritual through a violently delightful orgasm. That was four years ago, and here I stood pondering the future of my relationship.

After enjoying breakfast with Jericho and Kayla, I tried to busy myself to avoid Ahmad. He'd called and texted several times, which at this point, I found odd. Why blow my shit up when you have the no-name chick with the jacked-up house waiting in the wings? It was Sunday, so the boutique was closed, but I decided to do inventory and test some new oils. Bonafide was my happy place, my sanctuary. Climbing in the truck, my phone chirped.

Ahmad: Where you at?

Really? This nigga had the nerve to question my whereabouts. I was appalled.

Me: Heading to the shop.

Ahmad: Why? I thought you were coming to see me.

That comment invited my pettiness right in the door.

Me: Nah. I needed to connect with JD.

I kinda lied. And I kinda knew the mention of Jameson would piss him off.

The little dots danced for a few seconds, then disappeared, then reappeared. Ahmad was formulating a response. He and Jameson were... cordial. No more than a dry *what's up, man* was ever exchanged.

Ahmad didn't believe that a man and woman could be just friends, so he was always suspicious of our relationship.

The whole city knew Jameson 'Young Bull' Davenport as the local celebrity boxer from the wealthy Davenport family. But I officially met him seven years ago when his brother, Justin, owner of Davenport Realty, helped me find an affordable space for my boutique. I fell in love with an industrial space in Haven Pointe, just at the end of Main Street, but the owner was being an asshole about leasing the space.

"We don't need another damn salon in this area. I don't want my shit packed with a whole bunch of angry ass women." I remember overhearing the conversation between Justin and the owner.

I remember snappily sauntering to the front of the building, eyeing a much younger, brooding version of Justin leaning against the concrete pillar. The owner was his little brother, Jameson. Their father gifted the property to him as a college graduation gift to begin his career in real estate development.

After twenty minutes of cursing his ass completely out, I happily signed the lease after negotiating a lower price to include monthly massages. Over the two months it took for me to re-design the space, Jameson would leisurely stop by to help paint, build shelves, and bitch about what I was doing to *his* walls. Whatever I needed and some shit I didn't want, he did.

Although younger than me, Jameson was seasoned beyond his years, truly an old soul. What started out as a business arrangement morphed into a trusting friendship. I'd heard rumblings about his sexual exploits, but he never tried that shit with me. We just chilled. Smoked a little of his medicinally acquired weed, talked about growing our businesses, plans to buy more real estate in other cities, and traveling the world. He told me about the stupid shit these trifling ass girls would do just to get a taste of him, while I complained about lame dudes until I met Ahmad. Then I gloated over how romantic and amazing Ahmad was in our early months of dating.

The resounding ring through the speakers of my Grand Cherokee shook my reverie.

"Hello."

"You had to get up with Jameson. For what? That nigga claiming he couldn't sleep again? I don't like that shit, Giselle."

It took every ounce of decorum to keep my shit together. I wanted to blast his ass, lay all his shit bare, but I had to be strategic. I wanted to look directly into his eyes to witness the moment I broke him. With this type of man, it was a game of chess, not checkers.

"You don't like what, Ahmad? It was nothing, just his pain therapy."

"Ok. Yeah. Sure. Just pain therapy. When do I get my shit?" he fussed.

"Well, you've been busy. Unavailable to me lately, so..."

Ahmad's demeanor calmed slightly. "Never too busy for you, GG. I'll be at Mosaic downtown. Come through and have dinner with me tonight."

"Are you sure? I wouldn't want to disturb anything." I rolled my eyes.

"Baby, I'm asking my future wife to have Sunday dinner with me. Is that a crime?"

"No," I croaked. "No, it's not. I can be there around seven."

"Alright, baby. I can't wait to see you."

"Yeah, me too."

Three

"ONE. ONE, TWO. ONE, TWO, THREE." Jet's distinctive growl directed me through my weekly boxing routine. "What's going on, Bull? That shit is weak."

Sweat stung my eyes as I vainly endeavored to punch harder, faster. The pain coursing through my shoulder was like a collection of Ginsu knives stabbing me one after the other. This was just one of those moments when my body reminded me of the horrific injuries I'd sustained. It had been months since I experienced this level of stiffness and discomfort.

"Stop. Stop." Jet waved me off. "Your shoulder?" he questioned, and I nodded.

"Why you in my damn gym then, Young Bull? You trying to make the shit worse?" Jet tossed the equipment into the bin as he walked away.

His gym. I sighed, chuckling a little bit because Jet really claimed *my* gym, *Young Bull Boxing,* as his. John 'The Jet' Steward was a middleweight boxing champion who had been my trainer since I was thirteen years old. Being the youngest boy of the Davenport dynasty, I was somewhat of the reject. Unlike my brothers and younger sisters, if my parents said go right, I went left. I dismissed any and all directions from my parents, teachers, and coaches, until my father introduced me to Jet. He taught me how to channel my energy in the ring, and that was exactly what I did.

I was so good—skills unmatched. So good, I received a scholarship to Penn State University and trained for the Olympics. *Young Bull...* Jet gave me that name when I whupped on fighters six years older than me and inches taller who were talking shit. I was undefeated from thirteen years old until my twenty-first birthday, the day that forever changed my life.

"I'm good, Jet." I growled. "It's just one of those episodes."

"What's stressing you? What's on your mind?"

I sighed, extending my hands as he removed my gloves. Jet perched on the edge of the ring, and I followed.

"I don't know, man. I'm just ready to do something different, and I don't know what that is. I've been thinking about leaving Haven."

"Leaving Haven? What the fuck for? You are the damn prince of Haven. Your family is like royalty."

"True. But what does that really mean? People kiss my ass because my last name is Davenport, but so what? I feel like it's some other shit I could be doing," I complained, leaning against the ropes.

"Instead of fucking different bitches every night?" Jet's mucous-filled guffaw was the result of years of smoking after his professional boxing career ended.

"Why they gotta be bitches? And for the record, I don't fuck every woman you see me with, Jet," I clarified.

"Taking them flowers and shit but not promising a tomorrow." He lifted his brow in confirmation.

"Whatever, nigga. I will never promise tomorrow. They

get all of me in the moment. No promises, no expectations, no broken hearts."

"You taking the meds?" Jet changed the subject.

"Nah. I hate how that shit makes me feel. Gilly got me straight though."

I left Giselle's place around seven o'clock this morning after getting a few hours of solid sleep. Gilly had voodoo or some shit in those hands because I was guaranteed to be down for the count after her massage therapy. Calming music, candles, and the plush massage table were just icing on the cake. Giselle's ass had magic hands. During these painful episodes, she was my saving grace.

I peeked into her room before I left and thankfully, she was still sound asleep after a rough night. It pissed me off that Ahmad had her crying and pacing throughout the night. Was I surprised that he was cheating? No. But I was shocked that this dude was sloppy about his shit in these streets.

"Gilly, huh?" Jet's soft chuckle pulled me from my reverie. He arched a skeptical brow, standing from his seated position. "How long do you think *never promising tomorrow* is going to last? How long is that shit going to sustain you, Young Bull?" Jet didn't stick around for a response. I stared at him until he disappeared into his office and closed the door.

After getting stretched then showered, I dressed in distressed jeans, a black Supreme t-shirt, and black and white Air Force Ones. *I'm so St. Louis.* The epitome of *'I'm from the Lou and I'm proud.'*

Hopping in my Land Rover, I hit the button to open the panoramic sunroof so I could fully enjoy this rare spring day. Sunny and mid seventy degrees wasn't going to last long. St. Louis transitioned from freezing cold to hell in the blink of an eye.

"Hey, Jameson," a pretty little redbone whose name I couldn't remember sang as I walked into *Sliced and Diced.*

"What's up, shorty?"

"Nothing much. Just grabbing some lunch on my break." The no-name cutie bit the corner of her lips.

I ordered my usual—large turkey club spinach wrap, creamy chicken soup, and a cream soda.

"Add whatever shorty wants," I said to the cashier then winked to no-name.

She beamed, not even noticing that I had no damn clue who she was. Shit, did I fuck her and can't remember? That was messed up.

"Thank you, J!" she squealed, grabbing the brown paper bag as she closed the distance between us to whisper in my ear. "I've been hearing about that dick. Call me when you are ready to come through."

"I got you, shorty." I lied as she giddily galloped out of the door.

Thank God I didn't fuck her, I mused, ready to kick myself if I was that far gone that I couldn't remember. My mental rolodex was usually pretty reliable.

The owner of *Sliced and Diced* and one of my mother's good friends, Ms. Diane, shook her head.

"That dumb girl has no clue that you don't even know who the hell she is." She chortled. "Get out of here, boy."

I laughed.

"Have a good day, Ms. Diane." I waved, thankful I got in since the lunch crowd was forming.

My plan for the day was to check on a few new properties and head to my parents' house before meeting some business partners for dinner. Driving down Main, I spotted the familiar red and black two-toned Jeep Cherokee parked in front of Bonafide Beauty Boutique.

"What is she doing in the shop today?" I whispered to myself. Pulling behind the truck, I grabbed my food and headed for the front door. It was locked.

"Gilly?" I knocked but no answer. Knocking more aggressively, I shouted, "Aye, yo. Gil. Come on, man."

A fresh-faced, dressed-down irritated Giselle rounded the corner from the back of the boutique. I laughed as she shook her head once realization hit.

"What do you want?" Giselle planted a hand on her hip but didn't open the door.

"Stop playing, girl. Let me in."

"Nope." She popped her lips, stressing the P.

I couldn't prevent the grin on my face from her silliness. I raised the brown *Sliced and Diced*-logoed bag and cream soda.

"I got food." I figured bribery may work.

Giselle brightened, immediately opening the door.

"I got food but not for your ass." I cackled, quickly crossing the threshold before she kicked me out.

"You're an asshole, JD." She giggled. "What are you doing here?"

"The better question is what are *you* doing here on a Sunday?" I probed, following her to the office.

"You want the truth?" she asked, never turning to face me.

"Yeah, man. That's what we do. Keep it one hundred." I settled in one of the white leather chairs, placing the food on the small side table.

"I'm avoiding Ahmad," she whimpered, plopping into the other white leather chair.

I remained silent because I really didn't want to hear this shit, but I knew as her friend, I had no choice. Being best friends with a female was fucked up sometimes, especially for someone like me. I wasn't emotional. If someone fucked me over, I fucked them over. That was it, that was all. But Giselle was impassioned about everything. When she loved, she loved hard. But when she was done with your ass, she was done. Unfortunately, that wasn't where she was on her journey with

Ahmad. I had to accept the fact that she was still processing that her man was a fuck nigga.

"Oh yeah? How's that working for you?" I asked, unpacking the food. Giselle handed me a paper plate and napkins from the kitchenette outside of her office. I placed half of the wrap on the plate and slid it in her direction.

Giselle shrugged her shoulders in response to my question.

"Eyes on me," I demanded. "What are you going to do, Gilly?" I motioned my head to the sandwich, silently instructing her to eat.

"I wish I was a cheating type of chick so he can see how it feels." She bit into the wrap. "You always get the perfect wrap. Mine never tastes this good."

I snickered, shaking my head.

"I guess I shouldn't be surprised that he was cheating. There's no shortage of women in his face whether I'm present or not," Giselle continued, opening her mouth to accept the soup I fed her.

I remained placid. I was staying out of this shit unless she brought me into it. Gilly knew how I rolled. I was a no Vaseline type of nigga. Rugged and raw. Don't ask me shit if you don't want the honest-to-God truth. I felt those beautiful brown orbs glowering at me.

"You don't seem shocked at all." Her face was laced with unwarranted aggravation.

"Don't look at me like that. Direct that evil ass scowl in another direction."

"JD!" Giselle bellowed.

"You shouldn't be surprised either, Gil, because in your heart, you've known for a minute. Whether you saw his dumb ass in the act or not don't change shit. Cheating is cheating. You just gotta decide if you are going to tolerate it or move the hell on," I harshly blurted.

Shit, I didn't mean for it to come out like that. I hated to see her cry, and those doe-like eyes were beginning to overflow.

"Can I ask you a question?" she whimpered.

"Anything. You know that." Reaching across the table, I thumbed a tear away.

"Did you know Ahmad was cheating on me?" Those pretty brown eyes were fixed on me.

"I couldn't say for sure. I'd heard some shit. Probably the same shit you heard."

"You never said anything."

"Wasn't my place, Gil." I absently shrugged.

The silence between us was thick but not uncomfortable. Her innocently sweet, desolate voice broke my heart.

"I just want Ahmad to know how this feels." Giselle balled her fist, resting it in the center of her chest. "Because this shit stings." Her voice cracked, barely audible.

"Truth be told, I knew things had changed. And...I knew the wedding wasn't going to happen. Me and Ahmad have just been existing for the past year, especially once his mother died... Everything changed. But I was there for him through it all, and this is how he treats me. It's not even the cheating that bothers me; it's the lying and disrespect that is crushing me. If nothing else, I thought we were friends. And whoever this woman is... she's not a random fuck. Ahmad was familiar with that woman. Comfortable."

I gave Giselle the space to vent.

She muted for a long moment before she declared, "I bet if I did the shit he's been doing, he would blow a fucking gasket. He can barely stand me hanging out with you, and he knows we're just friends. Men can dish it, but they can't take it."

"Some men, baby girl. Some men," I corrected her.

"Whatever, JD. All the ass you juggle on a weekly basis is comparable to Ahmad's trifling ass behavior," she hissed.

"Nah, nigga, it ain't. I don't claim none of them chicks.

They know exactly what it is with me. No promises are made, and I damn sure ain't putting no ring on their fingers. If I do that, *when* I do that, all this other shit is a wrap. It's life for me. Contrary to what some may believe, I want a wife and kids one day. I don't plan to fuck around my whole life."

"Oh really?" Giselle lifted an eyebrow in shock.

"What?" I probed.

"That's a new revelation. I've never heard you talk like that before."

She took the last bite of *my* sandwich because she knew she could. Collecting the trash, I rose, glaring down at her.

"Yeah, well, maybe you don't know everything about me, baby girl." We locked gazes for an extended heartbeat before I disconnected from her dewy chestnut eyes.

Giselle slumped further in the chair, staring at the ceiling. She deeply exhaled, blowing the bangs of her wavy twists.

"I don't know what to do, JD." She unconsciously twisted in the chair.

"Sometimes a nigga gotta realize that you got options too. Two can play that game. But you have to be ok with the wins and the losses." I shrugged.

"Yeah, but he's cheating in the dark. If I cheat, I want to do that shit in broad daylight for his ass to see it all."

I tossed my head back, howling in laughter, but Giselle's face was fixed, humorless.

"Whatever you need, baby girl. You know I got you."

Four

"NOPE. Nope. Not that. Ewww, why do I still have this?" I complained, sifting through clothes in my walk-in closet, trying to find something to wear tonight. You'd think I was going on a first date with a stranger instead of dinner with my damn fiancé. It would, however, be the first time I'd laid eyes on Ahmad in ten days. Prior to him lying about going to New York, I was in Fort Lauderdale for a client's wedding, so we'd been on our grind separately for almost two weeks.

"Black jumper it is," I quipped, finding the perfect outfit to highlight all these curves.

Freshly showered and doused in my Bonafide branded citrus oil infused with rosehip, vitamin C, and shea butter, I pulled my three-day-old copper-highlighted finger coils into a high puff with bangs and applied a light sheen of natural makeup. Cute in the face and thick in the waist, with thighs, hips, and ass for days, thanks to my mother. My father gifted me five feet nine inches of length wrapped in reddish brown sepia skin. Gold leaf-shaped earrings, matching bangles, and black YSL Opyum sandals completed the simple, sexy, chic look.

I pulled my truck into the valet at Mosaic and was greeted by the little cutie pie Chris. At twenty-one, this boy was a flirt with way too much swag.

"I can die and go to heaven now that I've seen the beautiful Giselle Dean. Good evening, gorgeous," Chris greeted me.

"Hi, Chris. You know you are a charmer, boy," I teased, pinching his cheek.

"I told the boss man he better watch his back." Chris retrieved my keys then escorted me to the door. "Have a good night, beautiful."

"Yo, man. Ahmad gone fuck you up over his girl. Shit, she is fine though."

I giggled, overhearing the other porter whisper to Chris. I couldn't care less about these lil boys, but I must admit it was good for my ego to know I still had it.

"Hi, Giselle. Good to see you. Ahmad reserved your favorite table. Follow me," the hostess, Priscilla, chirped.

Mosaic on a Sunday night was a neo-soul grown folks vibe. Gemini, a popular local band, covered nineties R&B music while the customers enjoyed fine dining, the art gallery, exotic bourbons, and hookah. I ambled through the crowd, greeting folks I recognized from Haven. Even a few familiar glares from dudes I'd dealt with in the past were basically undressing me with their eyes.

Backless jumpsuit for the win, I mused, feeling myself just a little bit.

Priscilla guided me to the half booth positioned in the center of the club. It was truly the best seat in the house. Reaching the table, I noticed a bouquet of roses and my favorite rosé, *Lovie's Dream*, from the Toussaint Winery.

"Oh, this mofo is trying to show out, huh," I mumbled before thanking the hostess.

"Ahmad is dealing with a situation in the kitchen. He said to tell you he'll be out as soon as he can," Priscilla said.

I nodded.

I guess the damn kitchen was on fire because thirty minutes elapsed and still no Ahmad. He made sure to have all my favorite appetizers sent to the table though. Crab cakes, lobster tacos, and salt and pepper prawns. I was full of wine and seafood and honestly ready to go home.

Moments later, Ahmad's handsomely chiseled face, imposing frame, and panty-dropping smile meandered my way. He stealthily slid his lanky frame into the booth, immediately resting his hand on the small of my back.

Nudging me closer, he whispered against my ear, "You trying to get these niggas killed in here tonight. You are looking sexy as fuck, baby."

I cringed. My body stilled then winced, silently praying that he would let me go. The simple touch that would literally require me to travel with a fresh pair of panties, now made me... squeamish. The fact that the same hands caressing my thighs and the luscious lips kissing my neck were delivering pleasure to another woman just days ago disgusted me.

"GG, you ok, baby?"

I nodded, still wordless. Clearing my throat, I croaked, "Yeah, I'm good."

"I'm so sorry about the delay. Everything that could go wrong tonight did. Come here, baby. Give me a hug. I missed you." Ahmad clasped my hands, pulling me to stand. His solid frame lovingly embraced me as if he was truly lacking my touch.

I deeply inhaled him as I often did when we caressed. The Creed cologne that would instantly juice the seat of my panties, now did nothing for me. Nestled in my neck for a moment too long, he leaned back, surveying me before planting soft kisses against my lips.

"You coming home with me tonight?" Ahmad uttered.

"I can't. I have an early appointment at the bank, and the contractor is coming to hang the shelves in the shop," I blurted so fast as if I was lying, but it was all true.

"GG," he sharply groaned. "It's been over a month, babe."

"Don't do that. It's not like you've been knocking down my door to spend time with me." I rolled my eyes.

The audacity of this man to place the blame on me. While his manhood had been stroked by the no-name chick, my kitty was starving.

"You're right. I'm sorry. We've both been busy. I guess that's the sacrifice you make when building an empire."

Is this what building an empire was all about? Because if it was, throw the whole damn empire away. Externally, Ahmad Holten and Giselle Dean were the ideal couple. Men wanted to be like him, and women would happily murder me to take my place. I would destroy this empire to get a glimpse of what we used to be four years ago—struggling entrepreneurs supporting each other's dreams. Now, our relationship was all about Mosaic and Bonafide, no substance.

"Sure, Ahmad." I sighed. "Are you joining me for dinner, or should I get my food to go?" The blazing inferno mulling in my brown orbs did not go unnoticed.

Ahmad cupped my chin, forcing me to look at him.

"Baby, I'm joining you. Lennox just got here, so he can take over in the back. Give me ten minutes. Please." Ahmad kissed my forehead before disappearing into the crowd.

Shaking my head, I darted to the restroom to quell the discontentment brewing in my gut. I needed to woosah some shit before the bull-headed Taurus in me started turning over some tables in this bitch. I was so damn annoyed... with myself.

Entering the restroom, I glanced around, remembering when I decorated the champagne-colored space to give a touch of glam in the midst of the dark, rustic lounge. Washing my hands, I gazed at the reflection staring back at me, wondering how I got here. I hate that I expressed my emotions through tears. Happy, sad, angry, it didn't matter; crying was guaranteed. Deep inhales, audible exhales, and rapid blinking suppressed the impending sobs for the moment.

Exiting the bathroom, I smiled because the band was singing a cover of one of my favorite songs, Jill Scott's "Golden". The heavens knew I needed a little pick me up. I was snapping my fingers, mouthing the lyrics, and dancing my way toward my seat when two massive hands grasped my waist. The familiar decadent woody spice scent surprisingly provoked all my senses.

"Somebody got your lil ass out here thinking you cute. All your back out and shit," Jameson's slouthful drawl uttered.

"First of all, ain't nothing little about my ass. What are you doing here, JD?" I turned on my heels, scrutinizing his hazel eyes. They were narrowed and hazy.

I lightly chuckled because Jameson was high. Quickly eyeing him from head to toe, he was on his grown man shit tonight. Dark blue slacks paired with a paisley dress shirt rolled up to his elbows—no tie, platinum Cuban link chain, chocolate brown Gucci belt with coordinating dress shoes.

"Business." His one-word response was delivered in a gruff whisper. "And you?" he asked.

A gorgeous, petite Jada Pinkett Smith-looking woman dressed in an emerald-green dress approached us before I could reply.

"Jameson, our table is ready." She planted her hand on the curve of his brawny arm.

"I'll be there in a minute," he said, never disconnecting our gaze. The Jada-looking chick didn't move. Jameson's eyes furrowed as he turned to leer at her.

He sternly mumbled, "A minute. Please." She pierced an eye at me then nodded before strolling away.

"Your *business* is pretty." I smirked.

"It's not like that this time, Gilly." He pointed to the table where the woman settled.

Another petite but chocolate complexioned woman and handsome older gentleman were seated there as well.

"Double dating? That's not usually your style," I teased.

"Stop playing, man. I told you it's business. Their family is interested in partnering to revitalize some inner-city areas in Detroit and Indianapolis, so I'm considering it," Jameson explained.

"Nice. Boss moves." I extended my fist to pound with his.

"Boss moves," he countered. "I'll ask again. What are you doing here?"

"Dinner... with Ahmad," I whispered, slightly embarrassed because I knew Jameson was over whatever game I thought I was playing.

He smirked, nodding his head while eyeing me, annoyed.

"Don't look at me like that."

"Nah. I want whatever you want, Gilly." His brows danced, creasing the folds of his temple as he momentarily glanced over the crowd. "Here comes your dinner date now."

Ahmad crept behind me, snaking his arm around my waist and smugly gabbed, "Jameson, thanks for coming out tonight. I hope the accommodations are to your liking."

I squirmed as Ahmad caressed my hip, drawing me closer as he clutched the curve of my ass.

Jameson nodded.

"Ahmad. Always top-notch service," he uttered, then darted his eyes to me. "You all have a good night."

Hand in hand, Ahmad directed me back to our table. The waiter was delivering the main course as we approached. We simmered in uncomfortable silence for several moments.

"Did you know he was coming?" Ahmad asked, cutting into his porterhouse steak.

"Who?" I chirped, never looking up from my plate.

He paused, glaring at me.

"Jameson."

"No."

"Hmm. That's odd." He continued cutting. "You typically know each other's every move."

"Not this time, I guess," I scoffed, forking a piece of the delicious salmon into my mouth.

Silence. We couldn't even hold a friendly conversation anymore. The uneasiness settled over our table and loomed for what seemed like a lifetime. Neither of us were willing to address the enormous elephant in the room.

"I need to talk to you about something," Ahmad blurted.

Oh shit. Is this it? Is this the moment he reveals his secret? Is he going to tell me he's in love with the busty woman with the jacked-up house?

"I have an opportunity to open a Mosaic in Chicago," he announced. "I would need to move there for about three to four months."

I was so engrossed in my musing, bracing myself not to snap on this man, that the only words I comprehended were Chicago, move, and months.

"What? Chicago?" I testily questioned.

"Yeah, baby, Chicago. This is a great opportunity for Mosaic. Lennox would run things here, and we would hire someone for the Haven Pointe lounge opening soon. Since it's smaller, Lennox can oversee the operations for all locations."

"Why you? Why can't Lennox go to Chicago? He's the co-founder. It seems to me he would have some responsibility for the expansion," I grumbled, agitated by this entire conversation.

"Lennox is behind the scenes... operations. I'm the creative mind, the innovator, visionary. And let's be honest, I need to be in control from start to finish."

"And what about my plans to open another Bonafide location and expand my skincare products? That was supposed to be our next step." I actually crossed my arms and pouted.

"We will, babe. Not right now though. Mosaic is the new hot thing. There's no shortage of salons. We can do Bonafide anytime."

Wow, I mouthed, shaking my head in disbelief, more irked with myself than him.

"And what about planning our wedding?" I despised myself for the desperation in my voice.

"GG, let me do this, and I promise you I will give you the wedding of your dreams. Mykonos, Paris, wherever you want. Empire building... remember, baby?" Ahmad nestled my hands in his, kissing against the three-carat emerald diamond resting on my finger.

I gawked at his aesthetically pleasing features while the past four years frolicked in my psyche. I vividly remembered our late-night talks over Melvin's fried chicken and spiked lemonade, camped on the air mattress in his naked studio apartment, mapping our plans for Mosaic and Bonafide. Back then, the struggle was real. I was slowly building clientele, and Ahmad was managing a few restaurants part-time. But we did it, and I was honestly happy for his success. Our success. We quickly elevated, exceeding our own expectations for the businesses that were mere figments of our imagination just four short years ago. But we lost *us* in the process.

I snickered with a lazy, listless grin on my face.

"Empire building, huh," I whispered, taking a sip of my wine.

"Do what you gotta do, Ahmad."

Five

~~

"MR. DAVENPORT, I would really advise that you reconsider the surgery. The damage to the nerve is getting progressively worse. The surrounding tendons are applying too much pressure on the damaged nerve which causes the weakness in your left arm and tingling in your fingers." Dr. Lawrence Morrison was perched on the stool glaring at me, awaiting a response.

I blankly stared back at him. It was a Thursday afternoon, and I was at my quarterly appointment with my neurologist.

"That's not an option for me right now. What else can I consider?"

"Well, we can try a prescription strength pain patch. It likely won't have the side effects you experienced with the Percocet, but every patient responds differently. Continue with the massages and acupuncture since it seems to work for you. But slow down on the boxing training," Dr. Morrison stressed.

"But I—" I interrupted until he cut me off.

"I know, I know. It's your meditation. Keeps you

grounded. Maybe once or twice a week paired with more yoga and stretching. Okay?"

I nodded.

"Call me if you have any new symptoms or when you're ready to schedule surgery." He extended his hand for a shake. I obliged.

I winced in pain as I rotated my left shoulder before pulling my shirt over my head. The pretty chocolate nurse, who reminded me of Nia Long, knocked while simultaneously entering the room. She stood for a moment, glaring at the tattoo on my abdomen. The words *Faith Over Fear* were inscribed above my navel, along with a few others.

"Oh! Mr. Davenport. I'm sorry. I can come back if you need more time." The pretty nurse blushed.

I waved my hand, gesturing for her to come in as I fixed my shirt.

"Here are a few samples of the pain patch, and your prescription has been electronically sent to the pharmacy we have on file for you. I can show you how to apply the patch if you'd like." She bit the corner of her lip, flashing a pearly white Colgate smile.

"Nah, shorty. I'm good. Thank you though." Sliding off the table, I retrieved the samples and paperwork from her hands.

"My name is Dominique. You can call the hotline or my personal line if you find yourself in need of... anything." She shuffled her eyes to the papers in my hand. Her name and phone number were written at the top.

I tittered, saluting her with the peace sign before exiting the office.

I chuckled and shook my head thinking back on a time when Dominique would've been ass up and face down on the exam table. But that type of shit didn't fulfill me anymore.

Desperately needing air, I opted for the stairs instead of

the elevator. At twenty-eight years old, sometimes my body felt like an eighty-year-old man. Years of boxing and one stupid ass mistake was to blame. Tossing the box of patches on the passenger seat, I spoke. "Call Giselle." The phone rang but no answer. I tried again. Nothing.

"Text Giselle Dean," I blurted. *"Ready to text Giselle Dean,"* Siri instructed. Gil. Where you at? Call me.

I didn't anticipate my three o'clock appointment lasting for two hours. Now rush hour traffic was adding to my annoyance. When the phone resounded throughout my truck, I expected the screen to read *Gilly,* but it was my brother.

"What's up, Jeremiah?" I barked, a bit more harshly than intended.

"I'm good, bro, and how are you?" He sarcastically snickered. "What the hell has you so irritable? You bleeding, nigga? It's that time of the month?" Jeremiah jeered.

"Man, fuck you." I couldn't help but laugh. "Nah, just came from the neurologist, and he's still trying to get me to have another surgery."

"So, what's the problem?" he probed.

"The scar tissue from the last surgery is causing most of the problems I'm having. So, why would I get another damn surgery that could put me in more pain?"

"Or it could help, bro. That's a tough one though. I guess GG's magic hands don't work anymore," he teased me.

"Nah, Gilly is the *only* thing that works." I peered at my phone... Still no text from her.

"Huh? Nigga, that's a loaded statement. Be careful with that grown ass, fine ass, *engaged* ass woman."

"Whatever, bro. What are you about to get into?" I asked, quickly changing the subject to anything but Giselle.

"That's why I was calling. Me, Pop, and Justin are about to hit up Nate's new cigar bar. You coming through?"

"Yeah. If I ever get out of this damn traffic. I'll get with you in a minute."

"Alright, bro."

"Yep."

* * *

What should've been a less than thirty-minute commute took me over an hour in traffic. Our barber and friend, Nate Marloe, was having a grand opening for his cigar lounge, Flame, in a couple weeks, but tonight, he was hosting a sneak peek for a small group of family and friends. Nate was actually partnering with Giselle's ole dude, Ahmad, and his business partner, Lennox, on this project. Flame would be the lounge portion of a smaller version of Mosaic. Unlike the restaurants, the new location would offer a full bar, small bites, and an array of cigars.

Ahmad had been in Chicago for almost three months. Initially, Giselle was bitching and complaining about his departure because it made her mind wander. If he was going to cheat, it didn't matter if she was in the same house let alone the same city. But it appeared that now she was using this time to chill and focus on her business. I recently agreed to have her suite enlarged so she could have space for additional staff in the boutique. In her words, she was making boss moves and finding her peace. She'd even been a little distant from me. I hadn't laid eyes on her in over a week, and that wasn't how we operated, hence my discontent about not being able to reach her now.

Walking into Flame, I greeted familiar faces then landed on dark hazel orbs identical to mine.

"What's up, Pop?" I embraced my father.

"How are you doing, son? How was the appointment?" Pop whispered the last question.

39

"Good. I'm good. Some things to consider, but I'm good." He knew it was bullshit, but he didn't press.

John Davenport was my hero. I gave him a lot of shit growing up, but he never gave up on me and never compared me to my older brothers. He established very personalized relationships with my brothers and sisters that still continued. A real estate mogul in the Missouri area, he started flipping small houses in St. Louis city in his early twenties to rejuvenate the hoods. Then he began buying residential and commercial property all over the state, making millions in the process.

Pop taught us all how to grow our money in real estate. Me, Justin, and Jeremiah owned rental property and commercial buildings throughout the city. My sister, Jacobi, was a real estate attorney while her twin, Jaxon, was a finance guru, managing all the expenses for our family's businesses. It was truly a family affair.

"Ok, son. Take care of yourself. You know I got you whatever you need." He encouraged me.

I nodded.

Flame was fire—no pun intended. The rustic decor of Mosaic blended with the eclectic style of Flame was a match made in heaven. Sipping on cognac, my eyes glanced throughout the space, nodding at females, pondering if they'd shoot their shot. I hadn't been on no fuck shit in several weeks, so I'd had these chicks on ice for a minute.

I noticed Deeny and Nia from Vivre Salons, Tia from Bonafide, Laiya, Shay, and Bianca gathered at a sectional. All of Giselle's crew was in attendance, but she was nowhere to be found. I called again, texted, and FaceTimed her. No answer. I definitely wasn't going to question her girls on her whereabouts, but if I didn't hear from her ass by ten o'clock, I was sliding through.

I needed a massage anyway. All the testing and probing at the doctor's office aggravated my shoulder. As the night progressed, the soreness and numbing sensation got progressively worse. After my third Woodford Reserve neat and one Davidoff cigar, my buzz was just right, and I was ready to bounce.

Slowly climbing into my truck, I called Giselle one more time. Still no response. Now I was getting worried. I trekked to her house, favoring my left arm because my fingers were numb. Grabbing the sponge stress ball from the center console, I flexed my hand, silently praying that Gilly was good.

Parking in the driveway, I walked up the three steps to her door but didn't waste my time ringing the doorbell. I unlocked the front door with my emergency key and pressed 0426 to disarm the alarm. Surveying her spot, nothing looked out of the ordinary. The glare from the television illuminated the room enough for me to see that she was asleep on the couch.

At first glance, I was scared as shit because Giselle was so still, she almost appeared dead. The subtle rumble of her faint melodic snore relieved my anxiety. I eyed her for an extended heartbeat, wondering what or who was the cause of the empty bottle of Prosecco resting on the sofa table. With the Kindle reader clutched against her chest and dark rimmed glasses slightly crooked against her pretty face, she shuffled, causing the heather gray spaghetti strap nightgown to creep up her curvaceous thigh.

"Gilly." I stood next to the couch, gently trailing a finger up and down the curve of her thigh.

"Hmm," she moaned, wriggling again. Her nipples distended against the cotton fabric. Goosebumps flared against her velvety skin as I continued tickling her flesh.

"Gil." My voice grew louder as I gently pinched her rosy cheek.

"What?" Giselle groggily whispered before slowly awakening.

Narrowly opening her eyes, she jolted. "What the fuck?" she squawked, scrambling to the edge of the couch.

"It's me, crazy. Calm down." Brow wrinkled in frustration and pain, I settled next to her on the couch. "What the fuck, man? I've been calling since five o'clock."

Brown eyes still squinted and somewhat confused, she rubbed a hand down her face then fixed the glasses before muttering, "What time is it?"

"Almost midnight. What the hell have you been doing?"

Giselle stretched, arching her back over the arm of the couch as she released an annoying high-pitched screech.

"Absolutely nothing, and it's been wonderful. What's up with you, JD?"

Her words quickly faded from her lips. The smile she adorned was replaced with unease once she comprehended my stressed expression.

Abruptly diminishing the minuscule space between us on the couch, she cupped the arc of my face.

"JD, what's wrong?"

"Man, I'm in so much fucking pain, Gil." I tightly closed my eyes, voice unrecognizable. The bass-filled drawl was replaced with fragility, angst.

Resting my palm at her nape, I journeyed my hand up the back of her head, fisting her curly tresses in desperation. My forehead enmeshed against hers, I begged, "Help me, Gilly. Please." I gritted my teeth through the pain.

Six

GISELLE HAD NEVER WITNESSED me in this much pain. Typically, when I unexpectedly invaded her space, requesting relief, I would be close to breaking but not broken. Tonight, I was completely broken. The unbearable pain won.

"Ok. Ok. JD, I got you. I'll take care of you, ok?" Giselle searched my eyes for understanding.

I nodded.

She stood, hovering over me, extending two hands to help me up from the couch. I tensely clutched my arms around the pleasantly plump folds of her waist. We ambled upstairs to the loft area where she kept her therapy equipment. Familiar with her preparatory routine, I leaned against the wall, awaiting further instruction. I'd been in this space several times before, but for whatever reason, tonight, I was clueless about what to do next.

Giselle's expression was staid. She was in healing mode as she mutely strolled toward me. Gripping the seam, she gently lifted my t-shirt, being careful not to further aggravate my shoulder.

I grimaced, and she rapidly whispered, "Sorry, sorry, sorry."

The room was dim except for the subdued white lights that decorated the space. The scent of lavender and smooth jazz danced around the room, immediately generating tranquility. I perched on the massage table, observing her effortlessly navigate the various instruments.

"I want to start in the chair today," she instructed, gesturing for me to change positions. "There's a new technique I've been reserving just for you." For some reason, her customary wink hit different tonight.

"The combination of ice, heat, and vibration will freeze and then calm the nerves. Then we can move to the table for the hot stones and acupuncture."

I nodded, not in a position to question her expertise.

I straddled the massage chair, settling facedown against the cushioned headrest. Giselle's touch was so damn delicate as she examined my shoulder, noticing the swelling.

"I had a doctor's appointment today. They had me doing all types of shit," I complained.

"Ah, now it makes sense why you're in so much pain," she declared.

I nodded.

"Let's get you fixed up," Gilly whispered, fingering my hair before running her nails against my scalp. That shit felt so good. Too damn good.

She retrieved the warm towel infused with eucalyptus and placed it on my neck. Heated Bonafide-branded lavender mint oil covered her tender yet firm hands. Sweeping left, then right, then a circular motion, the cooling sensation distributed an amorous chill through my spine.

Damn, her hands were divinely crafted. The touch distributed an immediate sense of healing throughout my nerve endings. Giselle had to be casting spells, practicing sorcery, or some shit. Tylenol, Vicodin, Percocet, not even weed subsided the pain like Giselle Dean's magic touch.

"Fuck, Gilly. That feels so good. It's already better. You need to charge a grip for this service," I practically moaned.

"You're just drunk." She giggled.

"Yep. And so are you. A whole bottle of wine that I'm sure was laced with vodka. You were getting it in, huh?"

"Something like that," she uttered.

"You wanna talk about it."

"Nope. Do you wanna talk about what the doctor said?" she probed.

"Nope."

"Then there you have it."

We chortled as she gently pushed the back of my head into the cushion. We settled into an agreeable calm. I deeply inhaled the lavender, hoping it would lull me to sleep and quell the unannounced pulsing in my dick. I'd gone too long without a release, and now my ass was misconstruing Gil's normal healing methods for salacious, sensual touches.

Giselle transitioned to the new equipment, starting with the cold therapy to compliment the cooling sensation of the mint in the oil. I quivered, not ready for the extreme cold. Five minutes later, the tool began to heat, melting the chill that previously existed. Slowly, meticulously, Giselle guided the tool from one shoulder to the other. Her body seductively swayed with the moves of a ballerina.

"I'm switching to vibration. It can be a bit overwhelming at the onset."

I nodded.

My entire body jerked from the tingling vibration. *Shit!* I mouthed, clenching my legs tighter, vainly attempting to tame my unruly dick.

What the fuck was going on? I had countless massages in this room, with these hands, and this shit never happened.

Giselle's citrus scent and plush, curvy frame pressing against my back wasn't helping either. The beads of her rock-hard nipples and plump round breasts resting on the back of my head were driving me insane. *Fuck!*

The abrupt silence stirred me from my salacious musing.

"You ok? How does that feel?" she bent to whisper against my ear.

Gilly was fucking playing games.

"I'm good," I quickly responded.

"Take your time, but when you're ready, move to the table and lay on your back." Her hushed tone was no different than usual when she was giving a massage, but goddamn, today, that shit was sexy as hell. My big grown ass was ready to bust a nut if she kept playing with me.

"I need a minute," I groggily mumbled.

Gil proceeded to organize more tools as I sat there trying to negotiate surrender with my expanding member. Almost five minutes later, my dick was somewhat ready to cooperate, so I moved to the massage table.

Giselle approached the table and covered me with a warm blanket. She then retrieved a silver tray with six stones, more oil, and the tiny acupuncture needles. She folded the blanket three times, resting it just below my waist. I noticed her surveying my body, examining each tattoo covering my frame, focusing on the words *Faith Over Fear.* She'd seen them before, but for some reason, tonight, we were both acting brand new.

Thankfully, I was covered from the waist down, because my backstabbing-ass penis would not stand down. Rubbing the hot stones against a towel, she tested the heat level on her arm before resting them on my shoulder.

"Is that too hot?" That damn breathy, lustful voice was at it again.

I shook my head.

Giselle rounded the massage table, standing at the crown of my head. *Oh shit! Now her pussy is damn near in my face.* She gently rubbed the stones against my skin, circling in a consistent pattern.

What felt like a lifetime was only a few minutes as I plummeted into a zone when the music transitioned to Jill Scott's "Crown Royal". I didn't have to open my eyes to know that Gilly was rocking to the beat because anything Jill Scott was her shit, especially this song in particular. I obscurely opened my eyes to peep her pretty ass lips mouthing the words.

♫ "I flip shit, quick slip, hip dip and I'm twisted

In your hands and your lips and your tongue tricks.

And you're so thick and you're so thick and you're so

Crown royal on ice, crown royal on ice" ♫

Giselle oscillated her hips to the rhythm and blues beat as she harmoniously rotated the hot stones against my shoulders. It was crazy how she created different patterns to address different pain points every time. Her fingers aimlessly stroked like a pianist tickling the ivory.

Captivated by the symphonic melodies, she grazed my nipples with the stones. The first time I chalked it up as a mistake. But the repeat offense let me know that it was on purpose. Gilly's ass was straight clownin'. She replaced the cooled stones for new ones so fast, I wasn't prepared for the heated sensation.

"Shit!" I breathily groaned. She momentarily paused, circling the table to stand beside me. Remaining placid, I felt the table adjust. My head was now slightly elevated to allow her to apply more pressure. And she did. With one knee on the edge of the table, she pressed harder, deeper, at a slow meandering pace.

My dick was just plain disrespectful and disobedient. The blanket was useless as my manhood ballooned, tenting the thin white fabric. The expanse of my length basically poked against her arm, informing her of his presence. I probably should've been embarrassed when I narrowly opened my eyes to see that she'd become aware of me... but I was not. Her wide, beautiful brown orbs darted from my eyes to my mans on repeat, not missing a beat with the massage. She sexily nibbled the corner of her lips, the rise and fall of her braless breasts becoming more erratic by the minute. Her womanly aroma simmered, enlightening all my damn senses.

Shit! What is happening right now? I'd known Giselle for years, and never had I ever desired her the way I did at that moment. Don't get it twisted, Gilly was bad as fuck—always had been. A stallion for real. Tall, thick, plump titties, fat ass, curvy hips. But that face... shit. Smooth sepia skin, dimpled chin, glorious beaming smile. Just effortlessly pretty.

I licked my lips because a nigga was drooling, desperate to know what that pussy tasted like. I'd bet a million dollars that shit was as sweet as that lemon fragrance perfume she wore.

Gilly's hands continued to traverse my body well beyond my shoulders. Still singing, she relinquished the stones, using her fingertips to trace the letters of my stomach tattoo, journeying lower. I had to stop this shit, or I was going to fuck my best friend tonight.

"Giselle." My tenor was deep and stern.

She ceased. Her uneasy quiver did not match the passion, shit, lust brightening her pretty brown eyes.

"If you go down that road, there's no turning back."

Seven

JAMESON'S *ROAD* looked like a long, hard, bumpy ride, and for some reason, I was suddenly ready for a new adventure. Was it Ahmad pissing me off earlier by questioning my whereabouts while he was nowhere to be found? Or the potent THC-laced gummies JD left here a few weeks ago? No. Maybe it was the bottle of Prosecco with shots of Tito's and a twist of lime that had me giddily traversing the peaks and valleys of Jameson's glorious landscape like I was on a damn safari. A bitch was ready to scream *Jumanji* three times so I could get lost *in him*.

I trailed my French-tipped nails down the serpent tattoo spiraling his muscular arm, then the *D* over his heart with the names of his parents and siblings inked inside. My favorite tattoo on the canvas that covered his delectable body was the boxing gloves with *Young Bull* inscribed and a single teardrop. I'd always wondered what that tear symbolized, but now wasn't the time to ask.

The beauty of Jameson's body wasn't foreign to me. I'd seen him fight several times, and I'd administered countless massages, but this drunken highness had me keenly focused on the arc of muscles and mass and man.

This man's dick was so long, it shot up, extended beyond the waistband of his shorts, teasing me with a game of peek-a-boo. I could see the mushroomed head, and it was thick, caramel, and sparkling from a hint of precum. I wanted to touch it. Shit, I wanted to taste it... so I did.

"Gilly, you're playing with more than fire. I'm a whole fucking inferno, baby." JD practically growled the words as his hazel orbs grew dark, narrowed... sinful.

I leaned down and tenderly kissed his wonderment before circling the swollen tip with my tongue.

"Muther-fuck!" he groaned.

Slightly peeling back his shorts, the beast was unleashed. I ushered the head further into my mouth, easing into it, attempting to process the enormous feat I had ahead of me.

Slothful, languid licks from the base and back up was my rhythm of choice before steadily easing his length in the warm coziness of my mouth. Jameson was big, so time and patience were critical to conquering this monster.

He loudly groaned my name as my head bobbed, falling into a satisfyingly crippling rhythm. I was ready to feast on his steeliness, gluttonous for the taste of his member to satisfy my greed. But abruptly, firm hands fisted the tresses of my curly mane, ceasing my chase.

"Nah, Gil," he ordered, swiftly lifting from the massage table, bringing me up with him.

Jameson gripped my hair tighter, crashing his temple to mine. Eye to eye, nose to nose, he examined me, studying the depths of my orbs for assurance—consent. Tortuous breaths alternated between us, his synonymous to mine. We held an intense stare for what seemed like an eternity. An insurmountable number of reasons why I should abort the mission capered in my head. *This is your best friend. You're engaged. But his body... his dick! Bitch, this is your best friend.*

I ignored the rational and demented ponderings, nudging his chin to bring his mouth to me. Gliding my tongue across the seam of his plump lips, he tasted delectable everywhere. We harmoniously deepened the kiss, meaning all systems were *a go*.

Eagerly, desperately, JD parted my lips, drowning my mouth with his tongue. The pace... oh my God, his pace was lazy, languid, and so fucking good. His nails massaged my scalp as we wantonly feasted, lustfully loving every moment of the chaos.

Jameson slid off the table, never relinquishing my lips. In an instant, he clenched handfuls of my ass, elevating these two hundred pounds easily. He was tender yet aggressive in his approach as he laid me on the table. I widened my eyes, shocked by his strength while concerned about his shoulder.

Reading my mind, he deeply mumbled against my lips. "I'm good, Gilly."

Suddenly, I felt a slight adjustment to the massage table. My lower body was elevated a bit higher than my head. Jameson was delighted by the voluptuous surprise of my complete nakedness when he journeyed his massive hands under my dress. He pressed my knees against my chest, making room for him to straddle the end of the table. Draping both thighs over his shoulders, my legs parted, leaving me naughtily exposed. Given my position on the table, I couldn't see what he was doing, and the carnal anticipation had me ready to combust.

This man kissed and licked and sucked from the tip of my manicured toes to the apex of my essence, rhythmically mimicking the unhurried beat of Maxwell's "This Woman's Work". His firm hands kneaded the inner curve of my thighs while his sloppy kisses to the back of my legs ended with mouthwateringly violent bites that were guaranteed to leave marks.

I was never the type of woman to be inaudible during sex, always comfortably praising my lover when he was tapping this ass correctly while also unafraid to instruct my partner when he was failing miserably. But I was oddly hushed because Jameson required no guidance. He traversed my body as if he'd dwelled here before. Like I was *home* for him. Jameson may have been five years my junior by age, but this man was an ancient Herculean God with this tongue.

"Shit!" I finally bellowed as he palmed the plumpness of my clit, massaging, kneading, fondling. *Oh my Lord!* He leaned down with my big ass thighs still draped over his shoulders. This nasty mutherfucker licked from the crease of my ass all the way to my pulsing bud. How was he so flexible? Why was this shit so damn satisfying? I wasn't going to last long. No way, no how. Not at this pace. Not with his heated tongue puncturing my womb.

"JD! My God!" My back jetted from the table as if I was being resuscitated.

Somebody needed to call 911 because it was about to be a burglary and homicide. I was officially charging Jameson Edward Davenport with murder in the first degree and armed criminal action because he'd stolen every ounce of my common sense and was murdering my pussy.

I gasped, pouting as he temporarily released my clit. Snaking that damn tongue along my private lips, he glided both hands under my butt, resting them on the small of my back, deepening the arch.

Oh shit. My ass. He was licking my ass. I had never experienced no shit like that before in my life, and I wasn't a novice in the sheets. The sensation was too much. My head was pounding and spinning and pounding. Could it be the weed and alcohol? *No, bitch.* It was the up, down, in, out pattern, coupled with the guttural groan he'd chosen to dispatch on repeat.

"JD. The fuck—"

I had something important to say, but that shit was quickly lost when he flattened his tongue, licking from one end of me to the other, over and over again.

"Mmmhmm. How many licks does it take?" he taunted, drinking my shit like a damn Slurpee.

I was confused, disoriented, pushing against his forehead, begging for him to release me with one hand while clutching the back of his head, guiding him deeper with the other. I needed help.

Where the fuck is 911?

As the resounding tempo changed to Marsha Ambrosius' "Late Nights, Early Mornings", Jameson transitioned his choreography. Tongue up, down, in and out of my ass, while what felt like two meaty fingers swam in and out and in and out of my ocean.

"Jameson. Davenport. Goddammit, boy!"

I came so hard that I knocked every hot stone and every single acupuncture needle off the side table, grabbing for imaginary shit, anything to save me. Puffy little clouds formed in the whites of my eyes as they cuddled with the birds and bees. My ass had gone crazy—straight looney tunes.

Jameson granted me permission to bask in this gloriously violent moment. Softly, tenderly kissing against my stomach, his skin glistened with my juices. He lazed there for a long minute. Jameson was completely calm while I was experiencing sensory overload. Retrieving the remote control, he readjusted the table to its normal position. After several moments, my heart rate began to normalize, my breathing tamed, but my damn mind was in shambles. *My best friend just gave me the best orgasm of my life, and I want more. I want him. Shit.*

Eight

"JD, get up. Please. Get up now." I repeatedly smacked his back with the palm of my hand. I panicked, almost falling off the table.

"Gilly, what's wrong?" Jameson quickly transitioned, offering me space to hop off the table.

I scrambled, embarrassed, with all my ass exposed, unsure about how to proceed.

"Giselle, look at me. Baby, what's wrong?" he anxiously probed.

I momentarily paused, gawking at his dick. That thing was laying against the front of his thigh, fighting to be released.

"No, no, no," I quietly whimpered, frantically scrambling across the room, unable to navigate my own house.

"Don't call me that. Don't call me *baby*. That's not us. And put that thing away." I pointed at his dangling dick that appeared to be following me around the room. "This was wrong. JD, I'm engaged," I bemoaned. Still disoriented with a messy mushy middle.

Jameson paused his pursuit, apparently stunned by my words. I speedily darted down the hall to my bedroom, locking the door before he could get to me. Hectically pacing the length of my bedroom, I couldn't stall the tears any longer. I felt so stupid. Hair disheveled, skin flushed with my womanly nectar leaking down my legs, I felt like the dumbest woman on earth. Light taps on the door halted my rambling.

"Gil? Come on, man, open the door." Jameson's baritone was strained.

Silence.

"Giselle. Are you fucking serious right now? Talk to me," he begged.

More silence.

"You're just not gonna say shit to me, huh?" He pounded against the door one time.

"Good night, Jameson," I croaked.

* * *

7:06am. He didn't leave. There was no movement on the security cameras overnight, and his truck was still in the driveway. I honestly wasn't surprised. After everything that happened last night, my home was still his respite, the only place where he could sleep.

Although it was Friday, I didn't have a client until ten o'clock, but I needed to get out of here. I was suffocating knowing that Jameson was in the next room. Thankfully, I'd showered last night. Shit, I had no other choice but to shower because my juices were plentiful, and Jameson's scent was all over me—Tom Ford fucking Fabulous cologne mingled with cognac and cigars. His scent was not the only thing I tried to erase. Dark purple marks on my thighs, my ass, my breasts, even a spot on my calf. Evidence of his stately hands and magnificent lips were everywhere.

"A no-limit soldier indeed." I snickered, shaking my head with a slight giggle.

This shit was bad.

After too many minutes of unhealthy pondering, I reluctantly left the comfort of my bed to start my day.

A sleeveless maxi dress was the best choice to conceal the bruises splattered across the lower half of my body. I looked like I'd been in the ring with *Young Bull* for real. And damn, it hurt so good. The pleasure. The pain. Beautiful brutality.

Peeking out of my bedroom window, Jameson's truck still hadn't moved. *Shit!* I couldn't do this with him today. JD's direct ass would want to dissect the events, while I wanted to just simply disappear—forget that last night happened. But how could I forget the euphoria I experienced when his mouth touched mine or his fingers invaded my treasure? That shit would be on replay all day, shit, forever.

Slipping into my Tory Burch Millers, I fluffed my coiled puff and grabbed my Telfar shopping bag. As if this wasn't my damn house, I slowly opened my bedroom door and crept down the hallway. I eyed the closed guest bedroom door before tiptoeing down the steps. I would forgo my morning smoothie since I was on some sneaky shit.

Not bothering to straighten up my mess in the living room, I pressed the code to the alarm and exited immediately. Not even ten minutes later, the text message notification chimed on my phone.

JD: Giselle! WTF! Where are you?

The dots kept dancing.

JD: You really on some nigga shit.

More dancing dots.

JD: You sneak out of your spot to avoid me. Really? That's the shit we're on? I'm out, man.

My mother always told me not to speak if I didn't have anything valuable to say, so I didn't respond. What was I supposed to say? Sorry I was drunk and high and sucked your dick and let you obscenely ravish my body. I didn't want to be the typical cliche—a woman gets drunk, sleeps with best friend, wakes up with regrets only to realize she may love her best friend.

"No. That's not us," I spoke to no one but myself. "I love JD, but it can't be like that."

I parked my truck at the boutique before walking to the Brown Bean for coffee. Main street was already bustling with businesses opening for the day and patrons fulfilling their morning routines. The coffee shop was packed as usual, but I had a plug. Chris, the valet from Mosaic, worked the early shift at the coffee shop before his classes.

"Good morning, gorgeous," Chris sang, cleaning the tables as I irritably ambled to the back of the line.

"Good morning, Chris."

He closed the distance between us, peering over each shoulder before he leaned in whispering, "I can hook you up. What do you need?"

I whispered my order then discreetly gave him my credit card to complete the transaction. Chris was the breath of fresh air I needed. His little young ass was going to break some hearts with all that charisma and swag.

Ten minutes later, I sauntered into my boutique. It was serene thanks to the calming meditative music Kayla had piping through the surround sound speakers.

"Good morning, gorgeous," Kayla quipped with a beaming smile.

"Good morning, sunshine. You're here early." I tossed her an air kiss.

"I couldn't sleep, and Jericho had an emergency at the station, so I thought I would come in early to change the display before our meeting with Garrett about the new website," she chirped.

Kayla was the boutique manager in addition to a chef. She did meal prep and personal catering for various clients, but her business ebbed and flowed. Kayla was truly a Godsend. Thanks to her OCD ways, she kept the boutique organized.

Kay continued leisurely reorganizing the retail shelves before eyeing me with furrowed brows.

"What's wrong with you?" Kayla questioned.

"What do you mean? I'm good." I sipped my perfectly brewed cappuccino.

"Hmm. I beg to differ. Sis in love." She eyed me curiously.

"Are we still meeting Laiya for dinner tonight, or is my brother holding you hostage?" I nervously snickered, endeavoring to shift topics.

"Un-uhn, heffa. Don't try to change the subject. Something is going on with you." Kayla rested the bottles of lotion and oils on the table before continuing to survey me.

"GG! What is that on your back?" She dramatically pointed, pursing her lips.

I rushed to the floor-length mirror holding the smaller mirror in my hand to see what Kayla was referring to. Shit! Another mark of Jameson.

"Um, it's nothing. Just a bruise from the gym," I lied.

"Um, no ma'am. It's been awhile, but I know what a damn passion mark looks like." She placed her hand against her ample hips. "We still getting hickies in our thirties, GG? And on your damn back."

I was mortified. Slumping in the plush chair reserved for clients, I tossed my head back between my shoulder blades, wishing I was invisible.

"Now, as I recall, Ahmad's punk ass is still in Chicago. So, correct me if I am wrong, but I think my sis-in-love is creeping!" she squealed, more excited than she should've been about my potential discretion.

"Kaayyy! I fucked up," I whined, dramatically clutching my face in the palm of my hand.

"You fucked somebody? Who? Where? When?" Kayla sounded like a damn frenzied poodle or an out-of-whack owl.

"I didn't fuck him," I declared, gritting through my teeth, eyeballs practically bulging from my head.

"You didn't fuck who?" The corners of Kayla's lips curved.

I deeply sighed, lifting my head to glare at her. I never lied to my best sister-friend.

"I didn't fuck Jameson," I whispered.

Kayla's squeak echoed throughout the boutique as she gyrated while clapping her hands.

"You and Jameson Davenport finally did the deed? Yes, bitch!"

"Finally? What the hell are you talking about? Jameson is my boy. My friend. We chill. We kick it. That's it, that's all."

"Well from the looks of that big ass passion mark on your damn back, y'all did more than just kick it like friends last night. What happened, GG?"

"You want the long or the short version?" I sighed.

"Bitch, I want the truth."

I proceeded to explain to Kayla what transpired between me and Jameson. I repeatedly asked her to close her mouth and stop gasping every time I spoke about the recklessness of his tongue and the size of his dick.

"And you left? Your own damn house? Without talking to him?" She scrunched her chubby face so tight I couldn't see her eyes.

I nodded.

"You stupid." Kayla shook her head. "That boy ate your pussy so good, he had you running away from your own property."

I nodded again because I didn't have a rebuttal.

"He's far from a boy, but what am I supposed to do now?" I whined.

"Well, you said you wanted to cheat on Ahmad so... check." Kayla cackled, motioning her finger, signaling a check mark.

"Seriously, Kay. I probably just messed up years of friendship. A friendship I cherish by the way." I shook my head, rapidly blinking to prevent the mist forming in my eyes.

"Talk to him, GG. See where his head is at. Jameson is probably as confused as you are... especially since you left him at your house." Kayla smirked, shrugging her shoulders.

"One thing y'all do well is communicate. You walked away, so you need to go to him. You need to apologize." She closed the distance between us and pulled me into a hug as the bell chimed on the door.

"What does GG need to apologize for?" Laiya's nosy ass busted through the door.

"Her and Jameson almost fucked. But he licked that kitty so good, this bitch ran away from her own house, leaving him there with blue balls," Kayla blurted, placing her hands on my shoulders as she shook her head in disgrace.

"Oh, finally. I was wondering how long y'all was going to play this friend game. I would've been fucked that nigga," Laiya nonchalantly proclaimed as she stood next to Kayla.

"So, what that dick do?" Laiya asked, biting the tip of her lime green nail.

"Laiya!" I squealed.

"Is he really a no-limit soldier, or have these bitches been talking shit?" Kayla pursed her lips, eagerly anticipating my response.

My eyes bulged, laughing at my silly friends.

"No-limit soldier. I thought I told ya," I sang, mocking the classic nineties rap hit. We loudly roared in laughter.

"Go talk to him, Giselle," they chimed in unison.

Nine

THE BELLS on the boxing gym's doors chimed after business hours. Jet and a few other trainers had just left but apparently didn't lock the front door.

"We're closed!" I shouted, dimming the lights.

"I know. But can *I* come in?" Giselle's normal resolute tenor was subdued... insecure.

She looked so innocent and so fucking good. The high curly ponytail exposed that damn neck and shoulders that I couldn't stop kissing last night. The lagging rise and fall of her chest made her rotund breasts more pronounced. It sounded shitty, but her beauty manifested differently now that I'd tasted the sweetness of her pussy.

"What do you need, Giselle?" My tone, on the other hand, was disgruntled, pissed off, and hurt.

"JD, can we talk?" She unhurriedly traipsed across the room, perched at the bottom of the boxing ring steps, staring up at me. I was standing inside the ring, shiftlessly gathering equipment from the training sessions earlier.

"Make it quick. I need to grab something to eat."

"Tada!" she sang, revealing a white plastic bag filled with food containers.

"A fajita plate from Masa. Chicken and shrimp, black beans, no rice, extra peppers, and sour cream on the side... just like you like it. It's a peace offering." Giselle rested the food on both hands, extending it to me as if it was a prized possession.

She clearly had just come from her weekly dinner with Kayla and Laiya at the food truck park not far from the boxing gym.

"You can leave it down there. I'll grab it when I'm done. Thanks."

"You don't want the food?"

"I want the food, but it ain't bringing no peace between me and you." I narrowed my eyes, gawking at her.

"JD," she whined. "I'm sorry." Giselle placed her wristlet and the food on the edge. She climbed into the ring but maintained the distance between us—her in one corner, me in the other. It was about to be a brawl for the championship.

"Sorry about what, Giselle, huh?" I barked.

"I don't know. Last night. This morning. Everything!" Her shout echoed in the room as she intensely hunched her shoulders and fidgeted her fingers like a five-year-old.

"Nah. That's not good enough."

"I'm sorry about last night, JD. Being drunk is not an excuse, but things went too far, too fast, and I should've stopped it."

Giselle's words ignited me because I *wasn't* sorry about shit. I dropped the equipment from my hands and snappily darted across the ring, getting directly in her face.

"You left me, Gilly. No conversation, no argument, no nothing. You just bounced." I was so close, I was certain my breath muddied the whites of her misty eyes.

"I heard the alarm and said, nah, she ain't leaving like this. She betta be getting the fucking newspaper or some shit. Then

I heard the garage door. Man, you just left. When do we do that shit, Giselle?"

"I didn't know what to do. What was I supposed to say to you, JD?"

"You communicate like a grown-up and not act like a little ass girl," I practically growled.

She rapidly blinked, quelling the tears and anger that were simmering. But I didn't give a shit if she was mad.

"You knew what to say last night though. You got a fiancé, right? Ain't that what you said to me? Huh? After you fucking let me taste heaven, you got a punk-ass fiancé. That's what you said, right?" I angrily spewed in her face. She dropped her head, but I demanded, "Eyes on me."

A single tear escaped those mesmerizing eyes. I hated making her feel this way, but I was like a runaway train. The pause button was straight malfunctioning.

"I'm sorry, JD. Last night... it was a..." she croaked, the words lodging in her throat.

I depleted the nominal break between us, pinning her in the corner of the ring. My unyielding hands tightly gripped the ropes on each side, boxing her in.

"Mistake? Is that what you want to say? Last night was a mistake?" My brow lifted to the rafters.

She mutedly cried, unable to formulate words.

"Nah, don't tense up now. That's what you came here for, right? To tell me last night was a mistake but you still want to be friends. Huh? Is that what you want, Gilly?" I earnestly nudged her chin, forcing her to focus on me.

"Nigga, stand on all ten and look me in my face and say that shit to me," I demanded.

My nostrils flared and breathing labored. I was irate. What the fuck did she mean it was a mistake? That wasn't how I deemed the situation at all. In my version of the story, I kissed my best friend, and the shit felt more right than anything I'd experienced in years. Shit, ever.

The moment we kissed, my entire soul was at peace. A nigga was instantly healed. Giselle had always been a critical part of my happiness. But now, she was a *beautiful surprise* that I didn't know I needed until it was momentarily in my possession then snatched away in an instant. Now that I'd had *her,* I was hungry, greedy for more.

I seized her face with both hands, our eyes fluttering in an adoringly raging dance. Giselle's head collapsed, face resting in the palms of my hands as she wept. I tenderly kissed the top of her head, lifted her face to kiss her cheeks, then behind her right ear.

"What do you want, Giselle?" I basically moaned that shit. My emotions were on ten.

She shrugged, simultaneously shaking her head as she aggressively wiped away the tears.

"Talk, man," I bellowed.

"I don't know. I don't know how this happened. I don't know what I want."

I leaned into her face, my mouth settling against the corner of her lips. I digested every single exhale she allowed.

"When I kissed you, licked you... sucked that sweet ass, did it feel like a *mistake*? Did you want me to stop, Gilly?" I interrogated.

Giselle's breathing was strained, uncontrolled.

"No," she exhaled in a whisper, but I heard it, nonetheless.

"I guess you want me to be your little secret, huh, Gil?"

Never removing my lips from her face, I slid my hands down her back then pawed her ass through the thin fabric of the dress.

Unconsciously, Giselle lifted her leg, rubbing against my thigh. The Nike basketball shorts were no match for the strength of my erection.

I hooked her leg over my forearm, lifting her to straddle me. Pressed against the corner of the boxing ring, I kissed up her neck then nibbled against the fleshiness of her ear.

"Is this what you want from me, Gil?" I slithered my hands up her thighs, lifting the material that was keeping me from her sugary treasure. Sliding a finger down the seam of her thong, I stroked her slick folds, tickling her clit. She was so damn moist. Shit. Her gasp sounded more like a whine.

"You want me to devour your sweet pussy? Make you scream my name again and keep that shit a secret?" I glided two fingers into her essence. Her wetness doused my fingers, creamy saccharine goodness streaming down my hand.

"Ahh!" Giselle's head fell back against the ring. She panted, rapidly blinking her big doe-like brown eyes. Her hands desperately fisted the collar of my shirt with her eyes bolted tight. She covered her face to conceal her emotions.

Gilly was in her head, calculating all of the possible outcomes of this equation. I would be many things for Giselle Dean, but her secret was not one of them.

"Look at me, Gil. You know I'll do anything for you, right?"

She nodded.

"But I won't be a fucking secret or friends with benefits. I won't be the rebound nigga. None of that bullshit. I told you, once you took this road, there was no going back. I can't ignore the way your mouth felt kissing my dick, Gil. It's impossible to erase the way your pussy tightened against my fingers." I nibbled down her neck until I was nestled in the savory folds.

Relentlessly, mercilessly, I flicked two fingers against her clit, causing a goosebump-coated shudder. Tight, yet tenderly, I squeezed her bud between the same two fingers and my thumb. With each squeeze of pressure, she muttered a semblance of my name.

Squeeze.

"J."

Tighter squeeze.

"JD."

The tightest squeeze and gentle tug.

"Jameson. Shit!" Gilly's pants were erratic, hasty.

"I'm a selfish man, and I don't like to share my shit. You and this pretty pussy are now *my* shit, Giselle."

I gave a final squeeze before fingering her sodden center. Gilly was spellbound as she graciously rode every thrust until she reached a savagely salacious climax.

"Jameson. Shit. What the fuck are you doing to me? What the fuck are we doing?" She grazed my lips before burying her face into my neck, vainly suppressing her bewilderment.

"This," I whispered, freeing my pained erection from the basketball shorts, allowing my dick to kiss her watery private lips.

I glided my girth horizontally and vertically against her pussy before lazily, slowly occupying her glorious abode. When entering Giselle, I heard angels singing because I'd penetrated heaven.

"Fucking amazing," I bayed, instantly satisfied with just one stroke.

Gilly was so damn tight, so damn wet. I had to slow my pursuit; otherwise, I was going to bust immediately. Her walls were putting a death grip on my manhood, requiring me to rest inside of her saturated folds for just a minute.

Pausing, I licked from the rise of her cleavage up to her neck before delivering my tongue into her mouth. Giselle clenched her legs tighter, begging, urging me to occupy her depth. I proceeded one inch at a time, gradually reaching the apex then languidly expelling my dick, teasing her with the tip.

"Jameson! Shit, boy."

"Call me a *boy* one more time, Gil, and I'm fucking your

shit up," I warned, knowing I was going to tear this pussy up anyway.

Gilly felt like a damn thousand-dollar gel pillow partnered with fifteen hundred thread count sheets. Her pussy provided the perfect place to slumber.

"Shit. Shit. Shit, boy." Giselle's pleasure bellowed throughout the rafters.

She wanted to get fucked up, so I obliged. I bit into her shoulder before gulping a mouthful of her breast as I pleasingly pounded and pounded.

Gilly was a welcomed opponent in the ring. As a boxer, I was always lethal when I trapped my opposition in the corner. She was no exception.

"Giselle. Shit. You feel so damn good. A connection this exhilarating can't be a mistake, baby. Fuck," I moaned, surprised by my vocal expression.

I was accustomed to delivering thigh-aching, carnal gratification. The mesmeric sounds of a satisfied woman were fascinating, music to my ears. The rumors about me being a *no-limit soldier* were accurate. I enjoyed gladdening the vaginas of many women, but I didn't always fuck, contrary to the neighborhood myths about me. Now, I couldn't lie; my body count was extensive yet selective. I didn't run up in just anything. But Giselle was *the prize*, the championship belt that every fighter sought in his career. There was absolutely no way I was allowing her to knock me down in the first round.

Tears streamed down her exquisite face, and I kissed and licked every one of them away. Stroking, caressing, fondling, kneading, I was so damn close, so deep inside her depths that I breathed to the rhythm of her heartbeat. Gazing into her misty orbs, I could see her battling between heaven and hell. Our passion was so intense, I didn't give a damn about my pleasure. Giselle's rapture, her climax was imperative. I wanted her to experience and appreciate every inch of me—my manhood and my heart.

"Shit, Gilly. I'm cumming!" I moaned.

She nodded, wordless as her pretty brown eyes disappeared to the back of her head. Goddam she was so sexy.

"Cum with me baby, please." I was begging like a punk and didn't give a damn.

She nodded again.

Still pressed against the corner, I kneaded a handful of her rotund ass while firmly grasping her neck. Our bodies enmeshed as I beautifully battered her pussy until we harmoniously reached a savagely splendid climax. Our yelps echoed, producing the most lyrical tenor.

We exchanged deep exhales and inhales in complete stillness. Giselle attempted to move, but the quake from the aftershock ceased her escape.

"Slow. Slow," I instructed as her body slipped from the corner.

She adjusted her dress then bent to retrieve the destroyed thong I'd ripped from her flesh minutes earlier. Then she speedily, yet wobbly climbed under the ropes to exit the ring.

"Man, take it easy. Just step out slow. I got you."

As soon as Gilly descended, I scooped her by the waist, tossing her over my shoulder. I'd be damned if she was running away from me this time. She cooed, giggling as I motioned for her to pick up the bag of food.

Ambling to my office, I hit the lights, darkening the gym. I finally rested her on her feet in front of the bathroom outside of my office. Gil didn't look at me when she gently tiptoed into the restroom, closing the door. Several minutes later, she leaned against the threshold of my office, watching me. She appeared coy yet completely sated, undeniably gorgeous, and scared. Sitting at my desk, I was devouring the food Giselle brought me. I looked up, motioning her to settle on the couch.

We dwelled in a surprisingly cozy quiet for extended moments. Unable to finish my food, I wrapped up the leftovers before gulping down a bottle of water. I rose, sauntering toward her as she perched cross-legged on the couch. My eyes widened when I noticed purple marks peeking from under the fabric of her dress.

"Gilly, what happened?" I motioned to her legs.

"You. You happened." She smiled slightly.

I instantly fell to my knees in front of her, raising the dress to view the full extent of the damage.

"Tonight? This happened tonight?" I probed, unsure of when I caused the harm. I'd been so engrossed in captivating every inch of her body that I may have gone a bit too far, not realizing my own strength.

"Last night and tonight probably. But it's fine, JD."

"Nah, it's not. Do they hurt?"

She shook her head. "No. Not really. They look worse than they are."

"I'm so sorry, baby. Can I make it up to you?" I kissed her knee then licked the bruise on her right thigh, then the left.

She nodded.

Since last night, I craved the taste of her pussy, reluctant to cleanse her sugary nectar from my palate. I wanted her flavor to simmer on my tongue because I was unsure if I'd experience her again. But here we were, me diving, swimming, shit, drowning into her precious treasure, on the hunt to procure another appetizing orgasm from her honeyed center.

After I feasted and fucked for a second time, I snuggled behind Giselle, wrapping her curvy sexy ass frame into an intimate, cushy embrace. She was unstirred, tranquil. Our collective eyes were heavy from exhilarating sex and sleepiness. Giselle and I were drunk, faded from a natural high. I didn't want this shit to end, but I wasn't a stupid man. Her situation was complicated, and I'd already decided that I wanted to be a key character in her complication.

"Gilly?"

"Hmm," she sleepily hummed.

"Don't leave me," I breathed, then drifted into a painless, restful slumber.

Ten

⤦

"JD. Oh my God, boy, you feel so good."

"You wanna get fucked up, Gil. Shit. Baby, you're amazing. Don't leave me."

I roused, vigorously awakened from a delectably enticing dream of *him*. Entranced. Gleeful. Jubilant... and scared shitless was the only way I could describe my emotions when I left Jameson's gym. Seven whole days quickly slipped away since allowing Jameson to commandeer every single smidgen of my body. But I could still feel him, his imposing hands stroking my face, my breasts, my ass. Our lips clung in hungry, reckless abandon. The spicy zest of cognac still loitered on my tongue.

"Shit!" I hissed, stuffing a pillow between my legs as I twisted and turned in the bed.

My body was still enraptured by this man, a man who should be untouchable, off-limits to me. After destroying my pussy in the corner of the ring, he kissed and caressed every bruise. Laggardly yet deliberately kissing my private lips, catapulting me into a third orgasm for the night. I was begging for somebody to ring the damn bell, throw in the towel, because it was officially a TKO. My ass was down for the count.

It was as if our bodies were interconnected, tangled, and I couldn't detach. Jameson consumed every corner of my mind this week. Visions of his adoring stare gazing at me as if I was the orchestrator of everything right in his life. His velvety baritone affably whispering *baby* through a pleasured grunt caused my panties to soak each time it echoed. That one simple word flowed from his lips so fluently, and I had to admit I liked that shit.

"When a fine black man calls you baby. Whew!" I lowly muttered, still struggling in the bed to calm the tingle invading my treasure.

A hot shower and my favorite vibrating rose toy would have to satisfy me today. While he'd definitely tried throughout the week, I couldn't allow Jameson to ravish my body again. My head was already cloudy, and I was failing miserably at making sound decisions.

I meandered into the shower, sighing once the steamy heat touched my flushed skin. I tossed my head back, closing my eyes to allow the water to stream down my hair and face. Reflections of me and Jameson snuggled on the couch in his office pranced behind my lids.

We'd drifted asleep around two in the morning after JD dominated my body once again. After I vigorously trembled from a mind-altering orgasm, Jameson nestled me so warmly, whispering sweet nothings and sensual everythings in my ear. We aimlessly chatted as I traced the outline of the cross tattoo on his right hand.

"What does the teardrop mean in the middle of your boxing gloves tattoo?" I breathily inquired, eyelids listlessly shuddering.

Jameson audibly exhaled, burying his face in my neck

before softly biting. This man could simultaneously inflict gratification and pangs like nothing I'd encountered.

"I was at the top of my game. Number one in the country when I graduated from Penn and ranked in the top ten for the Olympics. I thought I was invincible. I'd train with Jet during the week, then on the weekends, I fought underground. Most dudes did that shit to make fast money. Me, on the other hand, did it for the clout. Just to talk shit and prove I could beat any mutherfucker that came my way." JD sighed, moving closer to diminish the already minuscule space between us. My ass was perfectly nestled against his semi-hard manhood.

"This one cat had been talking shit for weeks, talking about how he would destroy me in the ring. 'Young Bull ain't shit. Fighting in college is for pussies,'" he mocked. "That nigga put a challenge out, so I obliged. The night of my twenty-first birthday, me and a few of my boys went to the underground spot on the east side. Dude was there, at least three to four inches taller than me and just as stocky. He bounced around the ring like he was Ali or some shit. The bell rang, and I pounced. I beat his mutherfucking ass in the first round." JD chuckled.

"Me and my boys hung out for a minute, celebrated, kicked it. We were about to leave when I felt a cold, piercing sensation through my left shoulder. Then a second and third before I could even react. That simple ass pussy came at me with some brass knuckles. My shoulder was fucked up, but I guess anger and adrenaline allowed me to ignore the pain. I was beating his ass again while my boys were handling his friends. Fast forward less than twenty-four hours later, I was in surgery, and my boxing career was over. Even if I fully recovered, I would've been banned from the Olympics and professional boxing because the shit I was doing was illegal." He paused through a long eyeblink.

"So I allowed myself to cry one single tear when I lost my

first true love—boxing." JD trailed kisses from my ear down the curve of my face.

He nestled me so tightly, his body cloaked me like a second skin. I could feel his heart rapidly pounding against my back as my heart ached for him. The immense sadness and regret were palpable. After all the years we'd been friends, I never asked him about the origin of his shoulder pain. I figured he would tell me when he was ready.

"I'm sorry, JD," I whispered.

"Don't be sorry, baby. You take care of me, Gilly. You're the only thing that gives me some relief. Promise me you won't leave me." His sluggish, sleepy chatter was somewhat incomprehensible, but I clearly understood... Gilly, don't leave me.

Early the next morning, I stiffly shifted on the couch. My body had been blissfully battered, and I was feeling every twinge. Jameson was focused on the computer screen on his desk before he glanced at me and winked. I narrowly smiled, gingerly sitting up.

"You good?" he asked, brow furrowed in concern.

I nodded.

"The crew will be coming in a couple hours. We should head out," he insisted.

"Ok. What are you doing?" I released a high-pitched squeal as I stretched.

Jameson chuckled, shaking his head because he despised when I did that.

"Erasing the camera footage from last night," he nonchalantly responded.

It took me a moment to process what he said but once I did I blurted, "what? We were recorded last night? All night?" I lurched, grimacing a little from the achiness.

"Calm down, man. I'm the only person with access to the security footage. The cameras are only in the gym, not my office. Everything is deleted, Gil. No evidence." He sexily grinned, staring at the exact moment when his manhood pierced my throbbing kitty.

I sluggishly ambled toward his desk, new bruises apparent. "Oh, I have plenty of evidence, sir."

* * *

Exiting the shower, I shook my head at the recollections consistently playing on repeat. *Get it together, GG.* I encouraged myself, desperately needing to get through one day without being sultrily haunted by thoughts of Jameson. Standing in front of the full-length mirror, I examined my thick, voluptuous body. Thankfully, the physical evidence of his welcomed intrusion a week ago disappeared after many nights of Epsom salt baths. Draping in a plush white robe, I rested at the vanity to twist my hair before lathering with my citrus oil. Today was going to be hectic with back-to-back appointments, so I dressed casually in a pale-yellow linen romper, Gucci flip flops, and a Grace Eleyae satin-lined turban to set my twists for tonight.

I hopped in the truck and checked my phone. I texted Ahmad yesterday, informing him that we needed to talk, but I still hadn't heard from him. Our communication had been sporadic at best. *I'm busy* was our standard excuse to avoid the monstrous elephant in the room.

Pulling into my reserved space behind the boutique, my phone chimed.

JD: Good morning, gorgeous. Your ass is running late again?

Me: Good morning. Just a little bit. LOL

JD: No worries. Chris is bringing your cappuccino. Have a good day.

I brightened, captivated by how this man often fulfilled

my unspoken request, even before the unexpected shift in our relationship.

Me: You too. You're the best.

JD: I know.

* * *

June in St. Louis was brutal. Although the temperature was in the mid-eighties, the humidity was set on hell. Business was booming, with everybody getting their summertime waxes and lashes, and Bonafide body oils were flying off the shelves. The boutique was packed because the majority of ladies in Haven were getting dolled up for the annual Young Bull Scholarship Fundraiser. Jameson hosted a community fair and charity boxing match every year to raise money for college scholarships. His commitment to the cause was even more admirable after learning why he could no longer pursue his dream.

The packed day of events started with a fair. Local restaurants set up food stations, Davenport Realty hosted home buying seminars, and barbers from Nate's shop provided free haircuts to the kids. It was truly a Haven Pointe signature event. I even had staff at the fair selling Bonafide beauty products.

The evening festivities consisted of the charity boxing matches held in the parking lot of Jameson's boxing studio and an after party. Local and some well-known celebrities were guaranteed to be in attendance, so these chicks were preparing to be on the rich nigga prowl tonight. After getting weave down their back at Vivre salon, they'd head over to Bonafide Boutique for lashes, waxing, and makeup. My schedule was so packed that I was missing out on the daytime fun.

"GG, what are you wearing tonight?" Laiya asked while reclining in the chair, getting her eyebrows waxed.

"I'm not sure. I really don't feel like going. Y'all done wore my ass out today. I just want to curl up with a good book and drink wine until I pass the hell out."

"You know JD ain't gon' have that. He's probably in his feelings that you are not at the fair now." Kayla cackled as she shuffled through a magazine.

"You already know, Kay." Laiya joined in on the guffaw.

"Whatever." I rolled my eyes.

I hadn't disclosed to my friends what happened with Jameson after they irritably persuaded me to go and talk to him. For whatever reason, I wanted to keep that moment private, sacred, at least until I figured out what the hell was going on between us. Kay and Laiya knew me well enough to know that something was going on, but they respected my privacy enough not to pry.

It was approaching noon, and I'd already waxed and beat face number five with about eight more to go. Applying the setting spray to the client, I overheard chatter behind the curtain where my newest esthetician, Tia, was servicing a client.

"Girl, I'm just going tonight to see Jameson's fine ass. He needs to stop playing games and let me see what all the fuss is about," the chick behind the curtain chimed.

"What do you mean?" Tia probed.

"I heard that nigga is a beast in the sheets. Shit, you can see he's slanging a damn anaconda through his clothes. I have been trying to get at him for months. He's been real lowkey lately though."

"Yeah, I heard he's a beast with it all, honey, but it be the same chicks talking about the same shit. I don't really believe they've had no parts of that man." Tia chortled.

"Well, let my ass be the one to confirm or deny the *no-limit soldier*." The woman's cackle echoed from behind the curtain.

I didn't realize the scowl forming on my face until Kayla cleared her throat to get my attention. I eyed her, feigning an unconcerned smile, but that shit was so fake. She squinted her charcoal orbs with scrunched brows, mutedly questioning if I was okay.

"See, JD doesn't have any shortage of *people* giving him attention. He'll be fine without me there." I kept the phony smile plastered on my face until I disappeared to the storage room.

Jameson had often been one of the main topics of the boutique's non-stop gossip train over the years. I never contributed to the banter, often ignoring the babble about his sexual proclivities. But today? Today, that shit hit different. I was annoyed, somewhat riled and... jealous.

Sauntering back into the main area of the boutique, the subject had already shifted to some other neighborhood eye candy. I had a small break before my next client, so I decided to restock the shelves while I listened to Tia and Kayla decide what they wanted to order for lunch. Moments later, the bell chimed on the front door, and a gasp swarmed the room. I peered up to see three deliciously sexy men stroll through the door: Jeremiah, Jameson, and Titan. All of them exuded big dick energy, but there was something about JD's sexiness that couldn't be negated.

Jameson was holding a box that appeared to be filled with white Styrofoam food containers. His eyes were on me while all eyes were on him. JD looked deliciously sexy in a burgundy *Young Bull Foundation* tank, exposing the gems that were his chiseled arms and chest. White shorts hugged his athletic thighs, revealing muscular smooth legs covered with more artwork, while custom white and burgundy high-top Air Force Ones draped his feet. Simple diamond earrings and a Cuban link chain added to his appeal. Jameson was a masterpiece.

"Hi, Jameson," the ladies harmoniously sang.

"Ladies," he greeted them, unhurriedly ambling toward me.

The women proceeded to greet the other fellas while lustfully staring at these arousing men. Bitches were literally drooling. Tia even peeked her little head from behind the curtain to get a visual. Laiya quickly retrieved her boyfriend, Titan.

"Come on, babe. These heffas are thirsty." Laiya cackled, clutching his hand to pull him outside.

I, on the other hand, was temporarily immobile watching Jameson amble toward me. Fresh haircut, clean shave, and Tom Ford cologne had me in a daze. JD continued to close the distance between us, never releasing his glare on me. My heart dropped to my ass, I was so nervous. Could people see? Could they decipher the shift in our dynamic? Could they read that Jameson in fact fucked the lining off my pussy and I was slightly whipped? *No, let's be honest, Giselle. Your ass is completely dickmatized.*

Jameson's intense gaze resembled a man with a lot on his mind. He was on a mission to get to me. My eyes widened, faintly shaking my head, signaling him to slow down. Jameson didn't give a shit about my situation. I could immediately discern that he was primed to lodge his fat ass tongue in my mouth right then and there—fiancé be damned.

"What's up, Gilly?"

"Hey, JD. What are you doing here?"

"I figured y'all was ready for lunch."

I nodded.

"Thank you. We were about to order something." We silently regarded each other for an extended minute.

"Thanks, JD. I can take the box." Kayla's big ass smile was quite irksome.

I huffed, rolling my eyes as she dramatically cocked her head to the side, flashing all thirty-two pearly whites.

"Let me holla at you for a second," he requested, motioning his head to the back of the boutique.

Opening my office door, he held it ajar with one hand until I entered. Abruptly, he backed me into my desk. The momentum caused my ass to sit on top, knocking over a few items.

"Gilly, why are you ignoring me, man?" he growled, mushing my cheeks in the palm of one of his massive hands.

"I'm not, J. You've been busy, and I've been busy. We both have shit going on," I breathily muttered.

I despised the way his aggressive behavior caused a literal flood between my thighs. If I was being honest, I would not revoke his request to ravish me on this glass-top desk right now.

"I fucking hate that I miss your ass, man." He nibbled at the corner of my mouth, deeply inhaling. "I still smell you, baby. Nothing has tasted better since. Shit."

I swallowed hard, futilely attempting to regulate my breathing.

"Jameson. Space. You-you promised." I was stuttering.

"I know, man. I know." Opting to plant a kiss against my temple, he loosened his grip on my face then asked, "You good?"

"Yeah. Tired as hell, but I'm good."

Jameson backed away from me, desperately needing the distance just as I did.

"I bet you made a grip today though. It's packed out there."

I laughed. "You damn right."

"Boss moves, baby girl," Jameson quipped.

I nodded.

"What time do you think you'll arrive tonight?"

"I'm shooting for an early arrival, like seven thirty, so I can dip out," I declared.

"Dip out, huh?" Jameson paused, narrowed eyes intensely focused on me. "Alright, man, let me get back to it."

"Alright."

We mutedly gazed. Confusion, desperation, desire... and a little love danced in the open space separating us. He turned to leave.

"JD?" I whispered, then he lifted a brow. "Thank you for thinking of me."

"Always."

I observed Jameson briskly stroll into the boutique, prepared to exit before he was stopped by one of the patrons.

"Hey, Jameson. How have you been?" a pretty, light brown, petite girl beamed, extending her arms to hug him.

"What's up, Jaidyn?" he retorted with a side hug.

"Nothing much. I just got back in town and was planning to find you tonight. You wanna have a nightcap? Like after last year's party?" She winked then coyly, biting her bottom lip and trailing a finger down the length of his serpent tattoo.

I walked further into the main area, feigning oblivion to the interaction, when he slowly spun around, surveying me before returning his attention to her.

"Nah. I'm good. I have other plans. Good seeing you though, shorty." Jameson opened the door then suddenly paused.

"Gilly?"

I immediately lifted my head at his commanding tenor. My eyebrows raised, but I had no words while awaiting his.

"Eat your food, man."

I stood motionless, watching him disappear into the crowd on Main Street. I was in such a haze that I didn't notice Kayla standing next to me. She whispered through gritted teeth for my ears only. "Bitch, he fucked you good, didn't he?"

Eleven

I SCHLEPPED through the garage door of my townhouse a little after six o'clock. My ass was dead tired. During the short drive home, I contemplated how many ways I could tell Jameson that I wasn't going to make it tonight. *I'm sick. My mother needs me. The shop burned down. I don't have anything to wear.* None of the sane or insane excuses would do. I had to show my face. One thing was true, I had no clue what to wear to a *Pearls and Kicks* themed party. Checking the Ring security camera, I noticed a box on my patio as my phone rang.

"Hello."

"Hey, babe," Ahmad's gritty baritone resounded.

"Hey." There was zero enthusiasm in my voice. I was borderline apathetic.

"What are you doing? You sound sleepy."

"I just got home. Tired. I've been moving since seven this morning."

I stepped outside and reluctantly picked up the unmarked white box with a red bow.

"Busy day?" he probed.

"Yep. JD's community fair and boxing fundraiser is today, so you know everybody was out."

I slouched on the couch, carefully opening the box to reveal silver wedge Converse sneakers blinged with crystals and pearls.

"Are you going? Sounds like you need to stay home and rest."

"That's not an option," I hastily barked, not intending to have that much bass in my voice.

"Why not?" Ahmad's voice elevated. "Oh, never mind. It's JD's thing, so you of all people can't miss his shit," he sarcastically spewed.

"And what is that supposed to mean, Ahmad? He's my friend. I attend every year just like you have. But it's suddenly a problem because you're not here to go with me?"

"Whatever, GG. It's all good."

"I bet it is, Ahmad." I shook my head.

The comfortless silence was deafening.

My lips curved to a slight smile as I opened the envelope inside the box.

Copped you some custom sneaks for tonight so you wouldn't be wearing those uncomfortable ass stilettos. See you soon. JD

"Everything good at the boutique?" He filled the hushed space.

"Yeah. Two new hires started this week."

"New hires? How? The space is not big enough."

"I had the wall removed to open up that unused storage room. It was too big for supplies but perfect to accommodate two semi-private workstations." I shrugged as if he could see me.

"And when did you decide that? We haven't talked about it."

"It's not like you've been readily available to discuss anything related to Bonafide, Ahmad. You asked me to let you focus on Mosaic, so that's what I am doing. I have some interest from a few stores, so I needed help to free up time to concentrate on my skincare products."

"What contractor did you use? I could've found someone."

"No worries. It's Jameson's property, so he took care of it."

Silence again.

"Fucking Jameson," he lowly whimpered.

"I'm really not in the mood to argue, Ahmad. If you want to talk, then talk. And maybe try calling more than once a week. Otherwise, I want to rest for a few minutes before I have to get dressed."

The angst in my tone did not correlate to the beam on my face as I gawked at the sneakers. This dude had shoes made just for me to attend his party. Shit, I no longer had any excuses.

"Whatever, Giselle. I just wanted to check on you. I probably won't make it to the grand opening of Flame. I gotta handle some shit with backorders here. I'll call you when I can."

"Yep," I indifferently declared.

We ended the call.

* * *

I conducted one final check in the floor-length mirror before dashing out of the house. Dressed in a white front-twist crop shirt, asymmetrical denim skirt splashed with tiny pearls, the Converse wedges, and white YSL wristlet. It was always a good day when I could achieve the perfect twist-out. The chin-length waves were big and bouncing to perfection.

My phone chimed, and something told me it was Jameson. His text message simply read, **Gilly?**

Oh shit, I mouthed. It was after eight o'clock, almost an

hour later than when I planned to arrive, and I hadn't even left the house.

I text him back. **OMW.**

That was met with an eye-roll emoji.

Fifteen minutes later, I pulled onto the packed parking lot where valet was available. The main event fight was just getting started, so based on my calculation, I was right on time.

Jameson made a lofty investment of money and time into this event, every year. The massive boxing ring was positioned behind the building, with large strobe lights illuminating the ring and parking lot. Multiple fully stocked bars were set up outside and indoors, rows of chairs flanked the ring while the standing room-only crowd was positioned behind the metal gates. People paid up to $200 per ticket for this event, adding to the thousands of dollars in scholarships Jameson would be able to award to deserving students.

Strolling through the crowd, I spotted Jericho and Kayla at the bar.

"GG. You look so cute. I love the sneaks. Where did you get them?" Kay gushed.

"You're looking super cute, Kay. You thick with it, sis," I teased, ignoring her question.

"That's why I'm keeping her ass real close tonight," Jericho fussed, handing Kayla a plastic cup.

"What are you drinking, Kay?"

"Just ginger ale. Mr. Melvin's chicken wasn't my friend today." She scrunched her nose, placing a hand to her stomach.

"Eww," I joked.

"You want something, GG?" Jericho questioned.

"Just water right now."

We navigated our way through the growing crowd to find our seats. Jameson had already distributed wristbands to gain access to VIP. We laughed and greeted familiar faces as we ambled through the standing room only section. Finally arriving at our seats, I hugged my parents before acknowledging the entire Davenport family. Attempting to be as discreet as possible, I searched the crowd for Jameson, but he was nowhere to be found.

"Aye, yo. Yo." His throaty baritone resounded through the microphone, producing a tiny grin across my face. I turned to see him standing inside the ring.

"I want to thank everyone for coming out earlier today and to all of you who are here tonight. A special thank you to our sponsors and vendors. We couldn't make this night happen without your support. So far, with today's activities, the silent auction, and private donations, we've raised over sixty thousand dollars." The crowd cheered with excitement as Jameson continued.

"Yo. Yo, wait. But that ain't enough." The onlookers quieted. "This year, the Young Bull Foundation's goal is one hundred thousand dollars, so we got a little more work to do. You see the pretty ladies in hot pink t-shirts walking around... and the dudes are wearing pink too." He rolled his eyes. "They will be collecting donations throughout the night. All proceeds from the food trucks and bars will go to the scholarship fund. The silent auction closes at midnight. Now have fun and spend some money." Jameson rubbed his fingers together before releasing a hearty guffaw.

I noticed a slight grimace on his face when he climbed out of the ring. He was in pain but always kept pushing. Dressed in all-white shorts, a fitted tee, and Gucci pearl and studded sneakers, Jameson was a sight to behold. He leisurely strolled toward me with a sexy smirk on his face as he periodically halted to shake hands with supporters.

Dammit, why couldn't my center simmer down in his presence? Her betraying ass was tingling and throbbing and shit, craving his *everything*. I visibly quaked. *What the fuck is happening to me?* I pondered, repositioning in my seat as he approached.

Jameson extended his hand to elevate me from my seat. He clutched the small of my back, pulling me into his imposing frame for a hug.

"Damn, nigga, you sexy with your old sloth moving ass." He teased me, landing a kiss against my ear before he whispered, "You're stunning."

"Thank you." I blushed.

"What happened to arriving early so you can sneak out?" he probed, smirking.

"You know I don't have a *hurry up* bone in my body. But a bitch is still leaving. When you see that church finger, then you know I'm out."

"Nah, man, we about to kick it."

"I don't want to kick it. I'm sleepy," I whined.

"Say less. We can always go to your spot so I can put you to bed." Jameson nibbled the corner of his thick ass bottom lip.

"JD!" I squealed, peering around to see who was watching this awkwardly lustful exchange.

"I'm fucking with you, Gil." He chuckled, mouthing his next words to me. "Baby, chill."

Jameson summoned the waitress. "A Peach Lemonade and a Woodford Reserve neat. Thank you, sweetheart."

"Here, chew this." He handed me an edible gummy.

"Um, no sir. You are not about to get me fucked up. I drove."

"I got you. You trust me?" JD didn't wait for a response. He simply slid his thumb across my lips before mouthing, "open," then slipping the gummy into my mouth. *Shit, that was so sexy!*

· · ·

Two hours later, I was a nina-poppin', chickenhead fool on the dancefloor at the after party. The peach lemonade filled with peach-flavored Crown Royal and edible weed had me hella bent, so prayerfully, I would maintain my ability to make good decisions. Jameson was off somewhere being *Young Bull,* wooing partygoers to gain a few more scholarship dollars.

All night, I felt like someone was watching me. I was not sure why or who, but I often had this strange sense of ogling eyes on me. When Nelly's "Air Force Ones" piped through the speakers, the crowd went crazy. Everyone at this party was *so St. Louis*, and it showed.

Kayla, Laiya, and I were laughing and dancing when Kayla's eyes suddenly widened. I followed her line of sight to see a somewhat familiar woman intently walking toward me. As she neared, I recognized the busty, jacked-up house bitch that was with Ahmad. She'd traded her bra-length weave for a short pixie cut wig. While Kayla's orbs continued to bulge, mine squinted in acrimony.

"We can't fight, GG. *I'm pregnant*," Kayla blurted.

My head swiftly shifted to her, unsure if I wanted to cry with tears of joy or tears of outrage if this chick said one word to me.

"I'm good, Kay. I'm not fighting this girl," I paused, replaying her words in my head. "Pregnant? Kayla! Congratulations, sis. Why didn't you tell me?"

"Well, I ain't pregnant, so let the bitch start something if she wants to," Laiya thundered.

"Excuse me. You're Giselle, right? From Bonafide Boutique?" that bitch rudely interrupted.

"Who's asking?" Laiya hissed. Her little bitty ass was like a feisty chihuahua ready to attack.

"I wasn't talking to you. I'm talking to Giselle." The chick rolled her eyes.

"Well, we're talking to you," Kayla asserted. "And who the fuck are you anyway?"

The main person instructing me to stand down was turning up fast.

I quickly stepped in front of Kayla because if this heffa laid a finger on my sis, I was about to fuck some shit up.

"Well, I'm Mercury, and I need to talk to you about Ahmad." She motioned her coffin-shaped nail between the two of us.

Talk? Why did this heffa think she had anything to say to me? The angst firing in my eyes caused my flesh to blaze. I felt like one of those cartoon characters whose head exploded in flames.

While I thought I was good, I was unable to contain the wrath when visions of this bitch in her robe hugging my fiancé danced in my head. If my eyes were a gun, this chick would be riddled with bullets.

As I was about to speak, Kayla's right hand extended over my shoulder and slapped the shit out of the girl. My and Laiya's mouths dropped, momentarily stunned. Mercury vainly dared to reach past me to get to Kayla. I took the opportunity to open-hand push her in the middle of her flawlessly beat face, thrusting her backward.

"Grimy bitch!" I shouted, ready to leverage every fighting technique JD taught me.

I eyed Jameson and Jericho in my peripheral as they hurriedly jogged to us. JD stepped in front of me. "Giselle, calm the fuck down, man."

Instantly, I dodged my head as Mercury's hand suddenly came flying over Jameson's broad shoulder. He firmly grasped her wrist, turning to address her, while using his broad body to block my violent attempts to knock the hell out of that bitch.

"The fuck is you doing?" he barked.

"I was trying to be a grown woman about my shit and talk to her directly, Jameson," Mercury chimed.

"You don't have shit to say to her. Bounce, Mercury. I'm only going to tell you once," Jameson warned.

Does he know her? I froze, stunned. What the hell just happened? Does Jameson know this bitch? Did he know about her and Ahmad?

"This don't have shit to do with you, J. I know that's your *best friend.*" She motioned air quotes. Jameson summoned security, and they immediately scooped her up as she continued to shout, "But you know she deserves to know the truth!"

I remained still, standing behind him, motionless, begging the angry tears not to fall. Not here. Jameson spun around to face me. Contrition and indignation were written all over his face. Savagery and recklessness were scripted on mine.

"Giselle." He calmly whispered my name before extending a hand to cup my cheek.

"Don't fucking touch me." I aggressively yanked from his embrace, but he continued to pursue. "No. Do not fucking touch me, Jameson. Mercury, huh? You know her?"

All eyes were on me. I was trembling so bad I dropped my phone. He clasped a hand around my nape, drawing me closer to him, but I violently resisted.

"Gilly, please, man. Let me get you out of here." Jameson begged as I continued to combatively shove him. He tossed his hands up in surrender, allowing me to freely pound his firm chest until I was exhausted.

My lips trembled, tears salting the corners of my mouth as I screamed, "You fucking knew everything, didn't you!"

Twelve

"FUCK!" I howled, running toward my Land Rover.

When I bent to pick up her phone from the floor, Giselle dashed out of the party so fast that I couldn't catch up with her. And her gigantic brother, Jericho, ceased my chase.

"Nah, nigga, let her go. Kayla's driving her. She'll be fine," Jericho barked.

"I need to explain, man." I pushed against his stronghold.

"Give her some time, Young Bull." Jericho placed a firm hand on my shoulder.

"It doesn't take a rocket scientist to see that you love my sister. No, scratch that... you are *in love* with my sister. Everybody can see that shit. And truth be told, I ain't mad at it. I've seen the way you protect her, and it's all respect, Young Bull. But give her a minute."

I momentarily calmed but refused to let daylight break without talking to Giselle. Jumping in my ride, I heard my brothers shouting, "J, bro. You shouldn't be driving." Jeremiah caught my door before I could close it. "I'll take you."

"Nah, I'm good." I aimlessly stared out of the window.

"Real talk, bro. I'm good." I looked my brothers straight in the eyes, confirming that I was sober enough to drive.

Driving the twenty minutes to Giselle's house, I wished I would've choked the shit out of Mercury when I first saw her stroll into the party looking like she was ready to fuck shit up. I found out Ahmad was fucking with Mercury a few weeks before Giselle rolled up on him at her house. His dumb-ass truck could be spotted anywhere, so when I pulled up on the Ave to make a purchase, I spotted that dude coming out of her house. Mercury was fine as hell, but in the words of N.W.A., she was like a strawberry—the neighborhood hoe. At least that was her claim to fame back in the day. It seemed like she'd minimized her hoeish ways, but I guess that didn't exclude fucking with an almost married man. And she couldn't say she didn't know about Ahmad and Giselle; everybody knew.

I parked my truck on the street in front of Giselle's brightened house. I settled in the car for a long minute, pondering how the hell I was going to explain this situation. And more importantly, was she going to forgive me?

Knock, knock. I shuddered to find Jericho standing at my window.

"I thought I asked you to give her time," he growled.

"Like I said. I need to explain. Shit ain't what it seems."

He eyed me curiously, probably contemplating if he wanted to put a bullet in my ass. Jericho jerked his head, motioning for me to walk with him to her townhouse.

Kayla opened the front door, likely not expecting to see me.

Before I could say anything, Jericho fussed. "Kayla Dean, what the fuck you doing slapping some chick? You're pregnant. You're gonna make me put a bullet in somebody before this baby is even born."

Kayla's stern expression toward me quickly softened for her husband.

"I'm sorry, babe, but that bitch had it coming. I'll do better. I promise." She stepped aside for him to enter, but she put the gridlock on me.

"Nope. GG's on a rampage. You should probably just go," Kayla blurted, that stern scowl suddenly resurfacing.

"I ain't scared of her rampage. I've seen that shit before. Y'all can go. I got her. I promise. You have my word."

Jericho retrieved his wife as they exited the front door. Spinning to face me, he warned, "Remember what I said? It's a good look until it ain't. Fuck with my sister... and I fuck with you."

I nodded, returning his fist pound.

Crossing the threshold into Giselle's house, I could hear her stomping and cursing in her bedroom upstairs.

"These mutherfuckers got me fucked up. Talking about he's my friend. Friends don't keep a secret like that. He knew my man... no, scratch that... my damn fiancé was fucking that manufactured ass bulldog."

Kayla was right; Gilly was on some other shit tonight. I ambled up the steps and silently leaned against the doorway to her bedroom, watching as she unraveled. Crying and pacing back and forth, she was talking to no one but herself. She didn't even realize I was there... until she did.

Her rant unexpectedly ceased as she calmly then eerily muttered, "Get the hell out."

I remained still—just stared at her.

"JD, I can't do this with you right now. Leave."

Giselle crossed the room, pointlessly seeking to shove past me.

"J, move, please. I don't want to talk about it." She cried, arms flailing against my stronghold.

"Gilly, stop. Come on, man, stop. I don't want to hurt you."

She hesitated, misty brown eyes laced with injury, disdain.

"Too late," she rasped, slipping from my grasp as my hands weakened.

Her words were a blow to my heart. Harming Giselle in any way was never an option.

She'd relinquished the sexy crop top, skirt, and sneakers I gifted her for a red cotton spaghetti strapped dress. As she stomped down the steps, I eased down behind her, listening as she slammed doors and rattled glasses in the kitchen. I rested on the last step, leaning against the banister, observing her.

Curled on the couch with her Kindle, she sipped from a glass of red wine and snacked on popcorn. I guess she'd decided to completely ignore me as she started reading and continued sipping. I lounged on the opposite end of the couch as we settled in strained inactivity for at least an hour.

"How long have you known?" She whimpered, absently glaring at the Kindle screen.

"A few weeks before you."

"How? You fucked her?" Giselle harshly rolled her eyes to gawk at me over her dark rimmed glasses.

"What? Are you really asking me some shit like that?" I frowned.

"Don't act like that would be misaligned with your normal behavior, Jameson. She's right up your alley. Remember what you said? That your body count is high, right? Is... what's her name... Jupiter, Mars, is she a part of the number?"

"Why does it matter? This is not about me. This is about your boy—your bitch ass fiancé."

"You had me in these streets looking like a fool, JD."

Tears fell as she squinted her eyes tight, shaking her head in disbelief.

"*I* have you in the streets looking like a fool when *that* nigga is running up in the neighborhood hoe? But somehow this has become my fault." I shook my head. "Get the fuck outta here. That's some bullshit, man."

I suddenly rose, ambling to the kitchen to calm the hell down and get a Corona. Gulping down almost half the bottle, I glared at the back of her pretty little head, wishing I could just shake some sense into her stubborn ass. I returned to the living room and set my beer on a coaster, lifting her legs from the couch, draping them over my lap as I sat down.

"Look, man, you're not about to put this shit on me. I saw Ahmad's truck on the Ave a few weeks before you did, when I was picking up some weed. I didn't know who or where he was on the street until they walked out of Mercury's crib and got in his car."

Giselle attempted to recoil, but I firmly gripped her calf, halting her escape.

"Gil, I didn't say anything because it wasn't my place to say anything. You've defended Ahmad on all types of shit, so why would I think this would be different? I figured at some point, what was done in the dark would come to light. When you told me that you saw him at her crib that night, there was definitely no need for me to add fuel to the fire."

"What did she mean by I deserve to know the truth?" Giselle asked the one question I was hoping she would bypass. "There was something deeper in that statement. What are you not telling me, JD?"

I sighed, rubbing a hand down my face as I took another gulp of my beer.

"Ole girl came to my gym a couple of days after I saw them. Clearly, she'd recognized my car too. She came at me with some bullshit about approaching you to make you aware of her relationship with Ahmad. I told her *fuck no*. She knew a lot of shit though, Gil. About Mosaic, his plans in Chicago," I paused, audibly exhaling.

"What? Tell me," she ordered.

"She was going to New York with him to meet his pops before they went to the DR. So, your boy did go to New York, but Mercury was with him. Gil, she said he was planning on calling off the engagement."

"Wow. Wow." She slowly shook her head, nibbling the inside of her cheek.

"I have to be the dumbest woman on earth. My fiancé is having *more than* an affair—he's in a real relationship with this woman. And you, my best friend, knew this shit all this time," she leered.

My damn brows shot through the roof. I was confused by where this conversation was going. I leaned back on the couch, allowing her to continue this bullshit ass rant.

"And you fucked me anyway? How does that look, Jameson?" She dramatically shifted her head toward me.

"What the hell do you mean? It looks like a mutual decision between grown-ass adults. I didn't make you do shit, Giselle."

"My best friend learns about my fiancé's infidelity, and instead of consoling me, he fucks me. You knew Ahmad was trash, and you slept with me instead of comforting me through the bullshit?" Her face scowled, staring listlessly in the distance.

"I knew that nigga was trash long before anything happened between us. If I was just trying to fuck, Giselle, I could've pursued that shit a long time ago. The many nights we've fallen asleep in each other's arms, on this couch... in your bed, did I ever come at you with sex shit—ever disrespect you? No. The night of the massage was the first time we ever kissed in almost eight years of friendship. And please, let's not forget, *you* put *your* mouth on *my* dick, so..."

Shit! I didn't mean to be that harsh. I could see that the shit stung. Giselle ventured to quell the tears, but it was impossible. She was hurt, and I'd fucked up.

"Gilly, I'm sorry—"

She tossed her hand up, dismissing any further conversation. "No. I'm done. Please leave."

"What?" I hissed, brows frantically furrowed.

"Leave. Get out of my fucking house. And leave my goddamn key," Giselle slowly uttered. Her pretty ass was sitting there actually pouting.

"You on some bullshit, man. Who's the oldest, huh? Me or you? 'Cause you're acting like a little ass girl right now."

"Whatever, JD. Just go." Her demeanor was ambivalent.

I rose from the couch, hovering over her. Bending to close the distance, I firmly clutched her chin between my fingers, brushing the tips of our noses.

"Nigga, I did what I thought was best for you. That's it. That's all. No bullshit. But your ass is spoiled, Giselle Dean. Wanting everything your way, on your schedule. Life don't work like that, baby girl. But I love your spoiled ass, man. And I'll be here... waiting... when you're ready."

Gilly tried to deny me, but I sloppily kissed her ass anyway.

"And for the record, I did not fuck Mercury. I'm out, man."

Thirteen

SEVEN DAYS, nine hours, and countless seconds. That was how long it had been since I laid eyes on Jameson. And I missed him like crazy. Isolation was the temporary solution for my confused emotions. I hadn't left the house all week. My wardrobe consisted of plush robes and cotton nightgowns. I was sure that I'd gained five pounds this week since Mike and I, the DoorDash delivery guy, were on a first name basis. And I started my period, *thank God,* so I was a bloated, all cried out, dehydrated mess.

Tia took the appointments I was unable to reschedule, and I feigned sick so that Kayla wouldn't traipse her pregnant ass over here. I simply wanted to be alone. I even blocked Ahmad because, at this point, I was so done.

After hearing that Ahmad was in more than a physical relationship with Jupiter, Mars, or whatever her name was, I wanted to pack his shit up and give it to the homeless man that sometimes roamed Main Street. But I needed to see his face. I had to look him in his anthracite eyes and say *fuck you* to his face.

Jameson hadn't called or texted me, and I wasn't

surprised. Like me, he was stubborn and unflinching when he was resolute about his position on a particular matter. JD truly did not feel like he'd done anything wrong. Since I'd had some time to process, I reluctantly agreed.

I couldn't confidently say that I would disclose to a friend my knowledge of her man's indiscretions, so I understood his point. Now if it was my brother, Kayla would know it all. That shit would be good as told.

My heart was finally accepting all the signs I'd ignored in my head during this past year with Ahmad. His late nights and early mornings at the club. The women becoming increasingly more comfortable approaching him in my presence. The distance that lingered between us even when we occupied the same space. I could pinpoint the moments when things went wrong, when I was no longer enough for him... and the moment when I didn't care anymore, when he was no longer enough for me. Those days when I enjoyed being alone, or even worse, the days I only wanted to share with Jameson.

If I was being honest, my relationship with Ahmad was built on this urgency to build our empires—*plural*. And there was the problem. We were constructing soloed empires, not a joint dynasty where we won together. When the nostalgia of two young adults with a dream camped on an air mattress in a tiny studio apartment wore off, the relationship's foundation was nonexistent.

I incriminated Jameson because he was the easy target. I blamed him because I was ashamed to admit he was right. Terrified that what I was feeling for him was never about a rebound. The shit was real. I ached for Jameson long before he took residence in my treasure. Shit, I craved him. But not for sex, although I desired that too. He'd been critical to the merriment I enjoyed in my life. I had to cleanse my heart and speak my truth—*one day...soon*.

Glancing at the clock, it was a little after four on a Sunday.

The grand opening of Flame was tonight, and I really wasn't in the mood to socialize. Laiya all but threatened me, and Kayla promised to disturb my peace daily if I didn't get out of the house. As much as I loved a good drink and a savory cigar, I didn't want to face Jameson. Not yet. And I was certain he would be attending.

Since motivation was non-existent, I decided to take my time getting ready. Meandering into the master bathroom, I turned on the bathwater, adding various essential oils. I lit a candle and connected my phone to the Bluetooth speaker. Scrolling through Audible, I selected an oldie but goodie novel, *Safe with Me*, by one of my favorite authors, Stephanie Nicole Norris. Stepping carefully into the bathtub, I sank into the steaming bubbly water, getting lost in the melodious chords of narrators Wesleigh Siobhan and Jakobi Diem.

Mirages of Jameson frolicked in my head. I loved his sexy aggressiveness that was only a facade to mask how much of a sweet and thoughtful human he was. The way his nose dimpled when he released a guttural guffaw. The satisfied hum of his low husky snore when I massaged his shoulder. *His shoulder. I wonder how he'managing his pain this week*, I mused. Honestly, I thought I would hear him breaking into my house at some point this week saying, *fuck you being mad. I need to sleep.* I would've graciously acquiesced.

I soaked for at least an hour before begrudgingly removing my satisfied flesh from the cooling water. Panning around the house for another hour doing absolutely nothing, I was now rushing because I was late. *As usual.*

I eyed myself in the mirror, pouting because my disposition remained somber. And when I was in an ugly mood, I didn't feel cute. And not feeling cute typically led to a horrible night. The red crop top with matching fitted knee-length skirt would have to suffice to accommodate the *flaming red* themed party. Vince Camuto espadrille wedges and gold jewelry completed the look. I mustered up a modicum of energy to pull my hair into a high curly puff with bangs and just enough makeup to cover the dark circles around my eyes.

Arriving at Flame, I searched for a parking space on the crowded street. The heavens truly knew their child because a space was available directly across from the lounge. If I had to walk far, I would happily drive right back home. Joining the crowd, I walked to the entrance, eyeing Laiya and Tia.

"Hey, girls, hey." I greeted them with hugs.

"Hey, GG. You feeling better, boo?" Tia questioned.

"I'm getting there."

"Is Kayla coming?" Laiya asked, already bopping to the music resounding from inside.

"No. Poor thing has been having all day sickness with her pregnancy, and Jericho is working tonight, so she opted out."

I slowed my words while trying to determine why Laiya was scowling. Her brow dipped in a deep furrow before I could investigate the issue. Large, clammy hands clasped my exposed waist, kissing against my neck. I cringed when the scent of Creed cologne wafted through the air, attacking my senses.

"Hey, baby. Surprise!" Ahmad proclaimed, landing a kiss on my jaw because I was literally squirming like a tantrum toddler.

"Ahmad, what are you doing here? I thought you said—"

"I'm surprising you, Giselle, damn." He interrupted with an attitude. "I wanted to see you. It's been almost three months, and I had a little break in my schedule."

I stared at him incredulously but opted to remain silent.

Ahmad gestured for us to follow him to bypass the line. He was part owner, so VIP access was guaranteed. But I didn't want his hospitality. I wanted to be as far away from him as possible. I could not be held responsible if my hand went upside Ahmad's head just for simply existing in this moment.

Tia and Laiya were excited about the VIP section, so I yielded to prevent making a scene.

Flame was grown and sexy. Dark navy-blue walls contrasted with deep mustard and peanut butter-colored sofas and chairs positioned throughout the space like multiple mini living rooms. The VIP section was slightly elevated with sectionals for seating and provided a circular view of the entire venue. While the oversized humidor room was in the back of the space, it was the center of attention, with soft yellow lights creating a radiant glow over the expansive selection of cigars.

The place was packed with attractively melanated humans. I was vibing with a peach old-fashioned drink that the waitress recommended I pair with a mango-flavored cigar. My buzz was lovely, although Ahmad was endeavoring to ruin it. He stayed up under me with his arm around my waist and hand resting on my hip.

"What's good, fam?" Lennox uttered, leaning against the rail that separated the VIP section.

"Hey, Lennox. This place is amazing." Tia blushed, nibbling her bottom lip. We all nodded in agreement.

"Thank you, gorgeous." He winked before continuing. "Yo, Ahmad. I thought you were getting in earlier this week. Change of plans?"

I leered at Ahmad, not with anger but disdain. A strikingly sexy face that used to render me weak, was now like poison, killing me softly. It was clear to me that the only reason Ahmad prioritized this little visit was because Juniper, Mars, whatever her name was, likely informed him of our confrontation last weekend. I was sure the gossip train also apprised him of how Jameson defended me then chased after me. I rolled my eyes at him as if he could see me. Why wouldn't he just go away? Thankfully, Nate appeared, needing to speak with Ahmad privately, so he finally was gone.

I puffed the flavorful stick, blowing O-shaped clouds in

the air as I encouraged Tia to dance on Lennox. Instantaneously, I halted, feeling eyes examining me. I felt Jameson before I could visualize him. Surveying the crowd, our eyes connected, and my heart melted a little. I was hoping he missed me as much as I missed him.

He wore dark gray distressed jeans, a crisp white button-up shirt, black Gucci sneakers, and a black fedora. He was minimally iced, per usual, and a shadowed beard had begun to bloom in just a week. He looked so damn good emitting all that big dick energy. *Shit, this man is fine.*

Seated in the VIP section on the opposite side of the lounge, I was certain he was sipping on Woodford Reserve and smoking the most expensive cigar. Damn how I missed the savor of the spicy cognac on his tongue. The space was dusky, so I was unsure of how long he'd been there. We briefly made eye contact before he turned back around to converse with his brothers.

Ahmad had disappeared for the past thirty minutes while Jameson and I were unproductively striving to ignore each other. We failed miserably, stealing cursory glances and minuscule grins across the dim-lit room.

"Excuse me, ladies. Bathroom break," I announced, but it fell on deaf ears since Laiya was nestled with Titan and Tia was flirting with Lennox.

The path to the bathroom was dark, and the walk back was even darker. I scooted past patrons ambling through clouds of cigar smoke. Even through the woodsy tobacco aroma, I smelled the zest I'd grown accustomed to.

Gently snatching my waist, Jameson tugged me into his firm body and simply stared at me. Placid. Voiceless. Words were not required because his glorious deep hazel orbs narrated the story of a fortuitous love that was vanishing before truly materializing.

"Hey," Jameson lowly muttered.

"Hey," I whimpered.

"You good?" he asked as his fingertips fondled the small of my back.

"I'm ok. Are you good?" I inquired, the palm of my hand settled at the center of his chest.

Jameson regarded me. The short moment felt like infinity.

"Nah, nigga. I'm not."

Fourteen

I SPOTTED Giselle as soon as I stepped into the club. I also peeped that punk-ass Ahmad too. It was apparent that she didn't see me, and I wanted to keep it that way for as long as I could. Curiously eying her from my darkened position in the shadows, I wanted to see how Gilly interacted with Ahmad after what transpired between us. Was all the shit we'd done bullshit?

He was keeping her on a tight leash, real close, as if he knew somebody was watching. Giselle wasn't mine, but his hands on her body, those voluptuous ass, thighs, and hips that I'd just devoured, was pissing me off.

An hour expired before she finally caught my gaze, clearly flustered, but I could see the elation in the flecks of gold in her eyes. I was bullshitting myself if I thought I was going to be able to ignore her. Once she became conscious of my presence, we couldn't resist surveying each other. Giselle was a thick-ass, sexy-ass devil in all that red, and I craved just a morsel of her salacious evil.

Gilly exited the restroom, unhurriedly journeying back to

her seat when I snagged her, leaning my stately hardness into her regal softness against the wall. With squinted fiery eyes, I glared at her—no words, no movement. I was maddened and mesmerized at the same damn time. When she retorted with, *I'm ok. Are you good?* I tightened the space lingering between us, unable to arrest my indignation.

"You got a lot of fucking explaining to do, Gil, because I have a lot of damn questions. That nigga looked real comfy... real cozy *with you*, like he was *home*. I take issue with that, Giselle."

"Jameson. I—"

I interrupted her.

"Seven days. Eighteen hours. And too many damn minutes to count," I accented. My thunderous baritone caused her to shudder.

"What does that mean, JD?"

"It's been too long since I've laid eyes on you, Gilly, and the shit is fucking with me. Then I walk in here to see you drinking, smoking, kicking it... with that nigga. I told you I don't like to share my shit."

"JD, it's not what it—"

"It's not what it seems?" I interrupted again. "Is that what you're going to say? When I said that shit to you about Mercury, you weren't having it, but I'm supposed to accept that from you? Man, I'm done. I'm out."

I eased my hand from her waist, firmly nudging her chin before walking away. Giselle hooked a finger in my pants pocket, preventing my abrupt departure.

"Jameson, please. It's seriously not like that. Can we just talk?" she whined.

I had a love-hate relationship with that whine, only desiring it when I was ten strokes deep inside her sodden pussy.

Surprisingly, Gilly cupped my chin to bring my face closer to hers. Even under the dimmed illumination, I could see adoration in her misty eyes... and so could other people. But at the moment, we didn't give a damn who was watching.

"Look at me, J. It's not like that. That's not where I want to be," she breathily uttered, her lips so damn close I could smell the fruity flavored cigar.

"Where do you want to be, Giselle?" I countered.

"Giselle?"

Our heads jointly shifted in response to Ahmad's gruff inflection.

"What the hell are you doing?" he barked.

"She's talking. She'll be with you in a minute," I retorted. My tone was rigid, resolute.

Ahmad's brows clashed in anger.

"Nigga, what?" he shouted, aggressively stepping to me. I didn't flinch.

"Ahmad, stop. I'll come talk to you in a second. Don't cause a scene." Giselle darted in front of him, momentarily pausing his quest.

"Nah. Fuck that. I am tired of your fucking *friend* thinking he runs shit," he spewed at Giselle before turning to me. "She's *mine*, young buck, not yours." He shook his head.

I maliciously chuckled, brushing a hand against the stubble of my newly acquired beard.

"You sure about that, dawg?" I calmly hissed.

Ahmad's eyes practically bulged from the sockets. Instantly, he thrust toward me, roughly shoving her from his path. She stumbled, crashing to the floor, hard.

My eyes darted from Giselle on the floor to Ahmad, then everything went black.

The next thing I remembered was Lennox tussling with a bloody-lipped, red-face Ahmad while Nate, Justin, and Jeremiah vainly attempted to compose my madness. Young Bull was unleashed, and I knew the damage I was capable of imparting on this nigga.

"Yo, Bull. Calm your ass down, man." Justin double-handed pushed me in the chest. "You can't fight his stupid ass, bro. You trying to go to jail?"

"For him laying hands on Gilly? Hell yeah," I touted.

"So it's like that with her, bro?" Justin inquired.

"It's *exactly* like that. I will fuck all this shit up for Gil. Where is she?" My brother grabbed my shirt to prevent my pursuit. "Move, Justin, damn. I need to find her." I jerked away from his grip.

"Go outside, man. Now," my oldest brother, Jeremiah, ordered, and I listened.

Exiting the building with all eyes on me, I searched but didn't see her through the darkness. I walked outside with my brothers flanking me. Ahmad was still bitching and talking shit, but I wasn't concerned about him.

I immediately spotted Gilly perched on one of the wooden benches lining Main Street. Sundays were typically quiet on Main, but there was no shortage of onlookers from Flame. Laiya was sitting next to her while Tia was hovering above. She appeared to favor her right hand, circulating it with a grimace lacing her face.

"Gil," I called out, and she quickly shifted on the bench.

Her beautiful eyes were flooded with tears among other things. Angst, terror, and apprehension lived there.

I lifted a brow, mutely questioning if she was good. She nodded, mouthing, "I'm okay."

"Giselle, are you fucking serious right now? You don't see me standing here, and you addressing that nigga like *he's* your man."

Ahmad broke from the human fence Lennox and Nate

created. I thought he was coming for me, but this mutherfucker explosively bolted toward her. I immediately reacted, breaking my brothers' stronghold.

"Nigga, back up. Don't come at her like that," I demanded, obstructing his path to Giselle.

"Or what?"

"You put your hands on her again, and you'll quickly find out. You don't want this, dawg. Trust." I pounded my fists together as if I was in the boxing ring.

"JD, calm down." Giselle limped, settling in front of me.

She placed both hands to the sides of my face, but my eyes were fixed on Ahmad.

"Jameson. Look at me. Please," she urged.

"Are you ok? Are you hurt?" I briefly shifted my gaze, eyeing a swollen ankle and bruised wrist. My nostrils flared, maddened eyes back on Ahmad.

"No. I'm fine. It's not that big of a deal. He didn't mean it. It was an accident."

Wrath couldn't describe the firestorm brewing in my chest. Was she really defending this dude? The *same* simple ass nigga that had been cheating. The *same* person who just knocked her on her ass—accident or not.

"You're still making excuses for him? When are you going to wake the fuck up? Is this the person you're choosing to protect your heart?" I riotously pointed at Ahmad but never disjoined my leer from her.

"A man who just lunged at you like he was ready to beat your ass. Maybe I am the one that needs to wake up because this *feels* like some bullshit. Did you use me, Giselle? To piss him off? Is that what this was? What did you say to me that day in the boutique? You wanted him to know how it felt to see the person he loves with somebody else. Being loved by somebody else." I repeated her exact sentiments.

"That mutherfucker sees now, Giselle. I'm right here. Loving you. So now what?" I openly confessed. Shocked eyes intently stared at the dramatics like we were the stars of a soap opera.

She frantically shook her head, mouthing *no, no, no,* while fisting my shirt as I slowly backed away.

"JD, you know that's not true. I wouldn't use you. You know me."

"I don't know shit," I spat.

Pausing my retreat, I diminished the gap I'd previously created. My brain was grappling between coveting her nearness while desperately needing separation from this woman. She was driving me insane. The fucking cause and the cure.

Temple to temple, I craved her touch. Shit, I needed that shit like air. All this damn air was circulating around me, but it was worthless because I couldn't breathe without her.

I whispered against her lips, speaking for her ears only. I could still hear Ahmad bitching in the background as he observed exactly what Giselle desired for him to witness—her being loved by someone else.

"I told you I wasn't going to be a secret or your rebound. You either want me or you don't, Giselle. It's that fucking simple. Do you want him or me? Because, baby, I know that I *only* want you. But don't be with me because that corny ass nigga fucked up. Want me because I invade your mind every damn second of the day. Because only I can occupy the four chambers of your heart. Desire me because I'm the man who makes you feel safe. The only human you want to wake up to every morning and fall asleep fucking every night. The man you pray for and with, Gilly." I cupped her chin, forcing our lips to connect.

"Giselle, want me because I *fucking* love the shit out of you. If it ain't like that for you, then you can keep that shit. 'Cause I don't want it." I deepened the kiss, breaking the seam of her lips with my tongue. Salted tears, cognac, and cigars momentarily dallied in our mouths.

I reluctantly uncloaked her as she hesitantly released her hold on me.

"Fuck!" My yelp loitered the night air. Two fists balled at my temple as I ambled away, never looking back.

Fifteen

JAMESON LOVED ME, but he left me. I couldn't say that I blamed him. How could I defend a man that was having an affair and just demonstrated more rage toward me than I'd ever experienced in my life? Ahmad was completely broken at just the thought of me cheating. Until a moment ago, he had no real proof. But the way JD just kissed me and caressed me, our secret was revealed for public consumption.

"You been fucking that nigga all along. Your best damn friend. This is bullshit, Giselle. I knew it was bullshit four years ago, but y'all were convincing. When did he add you to his list of harems, huh? You do know he's fucked everything walking around Haven, right? Is that why you blocked me—making room for your *friend*?"

I listened to him rant for several long minutes about Jameson's sexual prowess, basically calling me a bitch and a hoe, belittling me right in public. Surprisingly, my demeanor was unfazed. Honestly, I didn't give a damn, but I'd be damned if I allowed this grimy, cheating ass mutherfucka to further disrespect me.

"When did you get in town, Ahmad?" I impassively questioned, interrupting his rant.

"What?"

"When did you arrive in St. Louis?" I clarified, slowly limping toward him, closing the distance between us.

"What do you mean? I got here today."

"Hmm? Really?" My brow furrowed suspiciously.

"Don't do that shit, Giselle. You blocked me. Did you fuck that nigga?" Ahmad's interrogation was erratic.

"Yes, I blocked you, but *Mercury* answered your calls, right? Since according to her, you've been in town since Wednesday, right?" My placid disposition was aloof, *scary*.

Kayla and Laiya were little inspector gadgets. They'd made a fake Instagram account to follow Mercury, unbeknownst to me. Her IG had been fairly quiet, until this week, apparently. She raved about her *man* being in town to *'finally handle some long-overdue business.'* Laiya had just shown me the post while we sat on the bench.

I aimlessly circled my wrist to ease the pain in my hand as I continued to deplete the gap.

"Did she enjoy New York? How about Mr. Holton... Did he enjoy meeting her?" His eyes bulged. "Ms. Micki often said that your daddy wasn't shit, so I guess the apple doesn't fall too far from the tree."

"Watch your mouth, Giselle. That's bullshit. I'm not doing this with you here. Let's go so we can talk in private," he spewed.

I boisterously, almost crazily laughed.

"Oh, now you want privacy when you've called me every name but a child of God in front of all these people?" I smirked. "You can dish bullshit, but you can't handle it when I call you on your shit."

"Let's go, GG," he loudly ordered, snatching my elbow.

"Aye, yo. You don't want to do that, nigga." Jericho slowly growled, leaning against the brown police truck with his hand firmly pressed on his gun. I didn't even realize he pulled up.

"Did you fuck him, Giselle?" Ahmad repeatedly, deliriously interrogated me.

"Fuck you, Ahmad."

That was all he was concerned about, did I sleep with Jameson? Ahmad didn't get it though. It didn't matter because this was *over*. I was done, done. By the expressions of the onlookers, it appeared they realized that the woman in this scenario, *me*, was fed up, and there was absolutely nothing that this mutherfucker could do about it.

"How long have you been fucking that nigga, Giselle?" he irrationally repeated.

"Maybe as long as you've been fucking Mercury, and God only knows who else," I spat.

"Giselle... don't play with me. Did you?" he shouted, unable to complete the thought.

I laughed, circling my swelling wrist, then nodded.

"Yeah, Ahmad, I fucked Jameson Davenport. Real good too!" I shouted, so close spit spewed in his face.

"I fucked around and fell in love with my best friend." A single tear made a path through the trail of dried tears as I smiled in realization.

Ahmad shuddered as if his jolting would scare me, but it only added fuel to the scorching inferno brewing. I'd handled myself like a lady for weeks, giving him pass after pass, making every excuse for his behavior. The past four years speedily flashed like a flipping comic book, then suddenly... I snapped.

Slap. Punch. Kick. Scratch. "Nasty dick ass nigga. Fuck you, Ahmad." He remained still, absorbing my wrath as I added to the damage Jameson had already done.

I was crying, kicking, cursing, and screaming, while

Jericho lifted me by the waist, creating minimal separation between us. I bet the crowd wished they had some popcorn and a soda, because this was must-see TV.

"So you been fucking him all this time. That young ass nigga. A fucking fuckboy." Ahmad roared as Nate maintained a firm grip on his arm.

"No, Ahmad. Not that you deserve to know, but I haven't been sleeping with him this whole time. We never touched in all these years. Never entertained the thought of anything between us. You have a lot of nerve to call somebody a fuckboy. Ha. Look in the mirror because JD is far from that. Jameson is kind, thoughtful, honest, and loving. He mended the heart that *you* broke, Ahmad." I hated that my voice trembled, despised my tears, because I didn't want to give him the pleasure of even thinking I'd shed a tear for his ass.

"J is... a beautiful fortune that I never expected, but everything I've ever dreamed of. And now... I'm a glutton, starving for that man because I can't absorb enough of him. So say whatever you want about me." I heedlessly snickered, unconcerned about Ahmad's feelings.

"It's like that one song I used to love by Chrisette Michelle. What is it called, Lai?" I turned to Laiya for an assist.

"'Blame it on me'. Girl, you know that's my jam. Say that shit is all my fault. Boy, you can say that she left you outside with a broken heart for all we care," Laiya sing-songed loud and wrong, ad-libbing the classic hit.

"Yep, that's it. So, you can blame everything on me, Ahmad, if that makes you feel better. I really don't give a fuck. You can tell your boys, your family, your daddy, whoever that I cheated. That I messed up. You can say it's all my fault, but as long as you and everyone else clearly understands that me and you—" I motioned a finger between us—"this shit is over."

I limped to Jericho, my aching ankle now completely

swollen. I fell into my brother's arms, seeking temporary repose and to calm his ass down before he shot somebody.

"I'm fucking him up, baby girl. Look at your wrist. Your ankle. He did this shit?" Jericho jolted off his car once he got a closeup view of my injuries.

"No. Jericho, stop. It's not worth it. I'm fine."

"Let me get you to a hospital, urgent care, something," he pressed.

"No. I promise. I'm fine."

"You can't drive on that ankle, GG. I'll take you home."

"No," I snapped.

"Well, where do you want to go?"

"Jameson."

* * *

The industrial building downtown was somber and obscure on the outside but beautifully decorated internally. There were only eight floors in the old office building that Jameson converted to high-end lofts. I traded my wedges for a pair of Jericho's socks he found in the trunk. I was in so much pain, but I refused to let the night end without talking to Jameson. Hobbling through the lobby of the building with Jericho's assistance, I entered the code to gain access to Jameson's floor.

"You sure he's ok with you just coming in like this? That's a dangerous move, baby girl. Anybody could be up here with him," Jericho warned.

"Well, if that's the case, then I know where I stand," I said confidently, but my heart was pounding in my toes.

I deeply inhaled, momentarily holding my breath as we reached the eighth floor. I peered up at the cameras, wondering if he could see me. I'd only visited Jameson's loft a few times and never ever used the code and key. Unlike him, I would only leverage it for true emergencies, and I believed tonight qualified.

I handed Jericho the key to unlock the gate then entered a second code to open the elevator doors that opened directly into the dimly lit foyer. Flameless candles and wall sconces brightened the path as I stepped further into the great room with Jericho a few steps behind.

Jameson held a glass filled with cognac in one hand and the remote control in the other. One muscled leg draped across the couch seat while the other foot was planted on the floor. He was slumped deep in the cushions, eyelids heavy. His demeanor was impassioned and threatening and undeniably sexy. A tank top and basketball shorts minimally concealed his Herculean frame. Orbs aflamed, he glared at me then darted his eyes over to Jericho. They simultaneously nodded, seemingly reaching a silent consensus for me to remain.

My brother kissed my forehead before nudging my chin, silently signaling for me to keep my head up. I softly smiled, watching him until he disappeared behind the elevator doors. For the first time ever, we tarried in dreadful muteness.

"Hey."

Silence.

I loomed, leaning on my left foot for support while we gawked at each other. My heart had beaten thirty-seven times, and four commercials played before he broke the placidness.

"What are you doing here, Giselle?"

"I, um, I had the key that you gave me. You said it's for emergency situations, and I think I'm in a little trouble. So I came here."

"What's your emergency?"

"I think I'm losing my best friend," I broke, softly crying as I stood before him fully clothed but extremely exposed.

"Gil, man, don't—"

I interrupted, tottering toward him in pain. His brow

wrinkled with concern as he was about to speak again, but I blurted, "I didn't use you, Jameson. I would never do that to you." The muted cry quickly escalated to a feverish wail. "I just needed you to know that, ok. I, um, I'll go."

I frantically turned around and limped away from him when, suddenly, I was swept up into his arms bridal style. He gazed at me for a second before settling me on the couch. I stared back as he gently elevated my foot on a throw pillow.

"I should've beat that nigga's ass," he mumbled quietly, shaking his head as he examined my ankle and wrist.

"Why did you get to fight him, but I couldn't?" I scoffed.

"Because it wasn't that nigga's time to die. If you hit him and he fought you back... I would've prepared for those four walls."

Jail. He would've killed just to defend me.

"Well, I got in a few good licks after you left." I chortled.

"Giselle! You wild as fuck, man," he snarled, shaking his head.

I shrugged, remaining hushed, eyeing him as he navigated to the kitchen, grabbing an ice pack, towels, Advil, and a bottle of water.

Jameson was still voiceless and barely looked at me. He gently placed the ice pack on my ankle, wrapping it with a towel, repeating the same steps on my wrist.

"Here. It'll help the swelling." He offered me the water and pills.

Uncontrollable tears continued to sporadically fall as I observed him. Reaching up to thumb away the tears, he gruffly uttered, "Man, stop all that crying shit. You know I hate that."

"Ask me again," I requested.

"Ask you what?" He absently propped me against the pillows to ensure I was comfortable.

"Ask me where I wanna be."

"I'm not playing these games with you, Giselle. You don't know where you want to be." Jameson dropped his head, staying perched beside me with his hand on top of the ice pack, soothing my ankle.

"Aye, yo," I called, mocking his voice.

He lifted his head.

"Eyes on me."

His smirk, which was almost a blush, made me smile.

Lifting up from the couch, I removed the ice pack from my wrist to cup the curves of his face. Surveying his eyes, torment resided there, and it devastated me.

"I don't want you to be a secret, and you're not a rebound. The choice is simple. I want you, Jameson Davenport. I want you because you invade my mind every hour, every minute, every second of every day. You are a permanent resident in my heart, my soul. I've felt seen, heard, safe, and protected since the first day I met you. You've allowed me to be a spoiled brat but loved me anyway." I chuckled as he licked, kissed, and thumbed away my cascading tears.

"I want to wake up to those delicious, sloppy kisses and fall asleep with that mammoth thing nestled inside me." We harmoniously laughed.

"I pray for you daily, JD, because I *fucking* love the shit out of you." I exhaled a breath I'd been holding for far too long.

Jameson rested his head in my hands, softly kissing my palms before he wrapped his imposing gentle hands around my nape, drawing me into him. His kisses were pillowy-soft, delicate, and provocative as hell. Jameson wantonly sucked my bottom lip before feeding me his tongue, and I hungrily feasted. This man leisurely made love to my mouth so tenderly, so delicately, so damn good that I had already reached the pinnacle. Beholding me, he stroked and caressed the arc of my face, relishing in the moment as if I was a figment of his imagination.

"I keep touching you, Gilly, because I want to make sure this is real. That you won't disappear. That you won't leave me."

"I won't. I promise. I missed you so much, J." I moaned as his balmy tongue trailed open-mouth kisses down my neck.

His head steadily motioned up and down with the rapid rise and fall of my chest as he nestled in my cleavage. With one hand, Jameson liberated me from the bra thwarting his attack on my hardened areolas.

"Ahh, baby." I moaned as he guzzled a mouthful of my plump breasts.

Jameson soothingly encouraged me to lie back on the couch. Fondling at the seam of my waist, he eased my skirt and thong over my hips, slithering kisses along the way. My panties were useless, soaked, yet I was dehydrated by my thirst for him. He paused at my puffy ankle, shaking his head, momentarily pissed at Ahmad's punk ass all over again.

Gingerly, he guided my injured wrist to rest on the couch cushion, settling the ice pack directly above my clit. I gasped, my body jerking from the cooled sensation. His hot mouth sucking my breasts coupled with the frigid temperature disseminated shockwaves through my core.

"JD, I need to feel you," I begged.

"I need to taste you more, baby," he lustily drawled.

Jameson plunged into my pussy with hasty conviction. All tongue, all lips, all man. Licking, sucking, slurping, his tongue happily harassed my dripping walls. Two beefy fingers were invited to the party, slipping and sliding along my dampened folds. I shamelessly drifted in and out and up and down to the cadence of his thrust, syrupy nectar flowing from me, nourishing him.

Immediately, tears drowned my eyes, powerless over the sensorial burden commanding my body. Jameson was eating me, but I was binging on him, under his control. I was cumming... *hard.*

"Baby! Sh-Sh-Shiiit!" I squealed, head dangling off the edge of the couch.

"Damn, Gilly, you always taste so fucking good." Jameson climbed the length of my heaving torso while licking my womanly essence from his fingertips.

He crowded my mouth with his *me*-flavored tongue. His lascivious moans would play on repeat in my dreams like the dopest R&B beat.

"Baby, what about your ankle and wrist? I don't want to hurt you. Not like before. The bruises." He cradled in the nook of my neck, rubbing his nose against my cheek.

"You didn't hurt me, bae. The pleasure and the pain, it was my privilege. You can't leave me like this, J." A bitch was pleading for the dick.

Jameson repositioned my sated, lank body, resting me on my side, protecting my injuries. I didn't give a damn about a swollen ankle and achy wrist. The throb between my legs was severe enough to merit a crisis, and he was the *only* remedy.

JD hovered over me, removing his tank and shorts. That damn hefty piece of equipment protracted right before my eyes. He stroked himself with no shame. This nasty boy knew he was working with a monster. I extended my hand to touch it. Fuck that! I wanted him in my mouth.

"Giselle, baby, no. I would become unhinged if you put that reckless ass mouth on me right now," he cautioned.

I blushed but was anxiously curious and a little afraid.

Jameson carefully climbed behind me on the oversized couch, lodging one arm under my head while the other gently tapped and tickled my clitoris. The thickness of his manhood pressed on my ass while the beat of his heart drummed against my back... Good Lord, the pairing was so damn intense. Divine torture.

He whispered, "open," as he draped my leg behind his body. My fatty private lips bloomed, eagerly anticipating his immeasurable intrusion. Without warning, his dick suffocated my pussy.

"Jameson," I bayed, soprano vocals singing acapella.

"Giselle..." He panted my name like it was oxygen.

"Giselle," he called again, requiring his next breath.

JD's motion was sedated, laggard. He slothfully nourished my kitty one centimeter at a time.

"Gilly, shit. Your pussy is fucking paradise. Can I give you all of me, baby? I promise I won't hurt you."

"Please," I adamantly requested, praying that I wasn't begging for some shit I couldn't handle.

In the boxing ring, I thought I'd experienced *all* of him, but apparently, I was mistaken, because the deeper he traversed, the more I lost my damn mind.

"Shit, boy. You are so damn big. I can't take it." I buried my face in the pillow.

"It's almost there, baby," he tenderly encouraged.

Jameson lusciously thrashed, pushing and prodding until he finally reached the summit. He coasted in and out of my ocean, mercilessly stroking and fondling my pussy. He dug his hands into my flesh, biting, piercing, nibbling against the plumpest parts of me. I mentally prepared for the impending marks that would paint my body tomorrow. I was his canvas, his work of art, and he stroked me with smooth, rhythmic, repeating elements.

My womb stretched to welcome his bulky imposition, blessing me with every single delightfully curved, girthy inch. Pound for pound, this nigga upped the ante. He was fucking like a heavyweight, and I was down for the count.

"Baby. Baby. Shit. I can't—"

"Nah. What did you call me? *Boy*?" He aggressively nipped at my neck. "I told you I'm fucking you up every time."

I fisted my own damn hair as Jameson pleasantly pummeled into me. Briskly, he snatched my hips, shifting my body to ensure I didn't miss not one damn iota of his dick. And I didn't. The man was relentless, pushing me to the edge of climax just to withdraw his monstrous mass from my walls.

"Dammit, Jameson! Baby, you are too much. Please don't stop." I begged to be seductively bruised. Pleaded for him to supply my addiction. Shit! Jameson was my drug and my pusher. But he teased me, drumming that python penis against my clit.

"Am I a boy or a man?" he sexily probed.

I was empty, vacant, yearning for his fulfillment. I needed to breathe. The lack of oxygen had me dizzy, and I desperately wanted to answer appropriately.

"You-you are so much more," I breathily whimpered.

The mushroomed tip of Jameson's manhood flirted between shallow and deep thrusts. He idled at the edge of my watery, leaking center, loitering there for an extended heartbeat before crowding my pussy with his plethora.

"Jameson!" I screamed, cresting, swiftly reaching my pinnacle.

"Tell me, Giselle. What am I?"

My narrowed orbs submerged with tears as my orgasm riotously peaked. But I was overwhelmed by so much more than his perfectly crafted thickness dwelling inside of me. Jameson's dewy hazel eyes brimmed with one single tear as we connected in the muted realization that this, *us*, was the glorious embodiment of unspoken wishes. But finally... he was mine, and I was his.

"You are... the one my heart has been searching for. My love. My best friend. The most *beautiful surprise*," I confessed in a raspy tone.

He snuggled into the nook of my neck, cocooning me in

an adoringly devoted embrace. He tenderly nudged my chin, motioning me to look at him.

Kissing then nibbling the tip of my nose, Jameson declared, "Nah, Gilly. No surprises. Just fate. Our destiny, baby. This shit was meant to be."

A Year Later

"NOW WHAT WAS ALL that shit you were talking at the restaurant?" Jameson growled, standing in the ajar passenger door, preventing my exit from his truck. We'd just pulled into the private garage of his building after dinner with Laiya, Titan, Kayla, and Jericho. This was the first time Kay and Jericho had been out of the house since the birth of their beautiful baby girl, Bellami, three months ago.

"Who, me?" I coyly pointed to myself with a blush. "I wasn't talking shit, bae."

"Nah, nigga, don't act shy now." The dangerous grin on his face was sexy as hell. "You was talking big shit to your girls, remember? *I got that boy wrapped around my finger.*" He mocked me.

But where was the lie? Over the past year, Jameson and I had been inseparable. He catered to me and anticipated my needs before I could even articulate them. Honestly, much hadn't changed about our relationship other than the daily, nightly, whenever, wherever, lusciously searing, thigh-aching sex.

"I—I don't know what you're talking about, Mr. Davenport," I stuttered, trying to prevent my giggle. "Can I get out of the car please?"

I vainly attempted to swing my legs out of the truck, but Jameson squatted a bit, clutching them, making me immobile. His imposing hands trailed up the curve of my fishnet-covered thighs. The short leather miniskirt allowed for easy access.

"You're not gonna let me out of the car, J?" My voice was small as I nibbled the corner of my mouth.

Nothing. Silence. His narrowed eyes and the lustful lick of his lips told me he was up to no good. Jameson cradled my hips in the palms of his massive hands, shifting my body toward him. He leaned his head into the car to kiss me. Soft kisses dampened my right cheek, then the left. Tender nibbles against my chin and the tip of my nose. Jameson paused, eyeing me for a long, adoring minute before a slight smile painted his handsome face.

"You know you done fucked up, don't you?" he questioned.

I nodded, eagerly anticipating the salacious punishment he was about to bestow.

Using the word *boy* to describe Jameson was guaranteed to get my shit fucked up. And I welcomed the beautiful battering. Jameson guided the minimal material of my skirt up and over my hips, ripping the fishnets from my flesh to reveal...

"Your nasty ass ain't wearing panties. Goddamn, Gilly." He growled the words before crowding my entire mouth with his tongue.

Those slow and sloppy kisses were going to drive me insane. But the way his long, thick fingers invaded the walls of my pussy were guaranteed to write my death certificate.

"You got this *what* wrapped around your finger? Boy?" Jameson grunted against the corner of my lips as he plunged two meaty fingers in and out of my ocean. "Huh, Gil?"

"Shit. Baby. Oh my God." I panted so loudly, I activated Alexa.

Did you say Oh my God? Is that a distress signal? I hope everything's ok.'

Everything was not ok. This man stooped before me and feasted on my pussy in the plush leather passenger seat of his one-hundred-thousand-dollar Land Rover. I flailed so frantically, my elbow honked the horn, hand started the windshield wipers, and somehow, SiriusXM started to play slow jams.

"You sorry for talking shit, Gilly?" He whispered against my clit before massaging it with his lips.

"S-s-sorry... not sorry," I teased through a boisterous moan.

He chuckled, still tugging at my clit with his teeth. "Your ass play too much. You like it when I fuck this shit up, don't you?"

"Yes, baby. Please. I'm cumming. I'm cumming. I'm... JD!" I shouted when his motion halted, extracting his fingers and tongue from my dripping puss. "Baby. Wha-what are you doing? Why did you stop?" My nostrils flared as I huffed breathlessly.

Jameson stood to his full height, licking my nectar from his fingertips, sucking and smacking like he was eating the damn Fun Dip candy from the corner store in the hood.

Resting both hands on the edge of the roof, he sexily swayed back and forth, dick swelling against his zipper as he uttered, "Nah... you need some act right. I'll be in the shower when you're ready to apologize." He winked then walked away, bowed legs fighting to make room for that monster crowding his pants. I watched as his back disappeared into the private elevator that led directly to his loft.

"Fuck!" I whined, peering around at my predicament— clothes disheveled, legs wide open, and pussy dripping.

Five minutes later, I ambled into the darkened loft. Wall

sconces dimly illuminated the path to Jameson's bedroom. I heard the shower water and eyed his silhouette moving around in the bathroom. Removing what was left of the dismantled pantyhose, I disrobed down to nothing before entering the shower.

Jameson's body was truly a work of art. Michelangelo couldn't sculpt chiseled perfection like him. This boy, I mean, man, was a godly creation.

He leaned two hands against the marble tiled walls, allowing the steamy water to stream down his head. That dick was still demonstrating its prominence, standing at full attention. Thick, firm, veiny, shit!

"You gon' act right, Gil?" he questioned once he heard the shower door.

I nodded, wordless.

Shortening the distance between us, I gently caressed his waist, kissing the center of his stout back. Jameson loved to end his kisses with a tender bite. I mimicked the wanton deed all over his back. Rounding his athletic frame, I journeyed my way to the front, tongue kissing his right nipple then the left before clutching his manhood in the palms of my hands. I double-fisted his dick with unhasty, leisurely strokes.

"You are all man, baby." I nibbled, kissed, and licked up his chest, pausing at the arc of his chin. Gazing deeply into his narrowed, gorgeous eyes, I planted soft smooches against his lips. "All man, J."

Instantaneously, I dropped to a squat, ready to tackle this curved anaconda. Jameson's skin was the color of roasted caramel, but his dick was rock hard, solid dark chocolate. Continuing the languid strokes against his manhood, I lustfully peered up at him, delivering satiny soft licks to the head. I was teasing him with faint kisses, from the tip down the base on repeat. I eagerly anticipated Jameson's hand to grab the back of my head because he was never afraid to supervise the direction or the pace of my mouth.

Planting one last kiss, I flattened my tongue and licked the length of him before swallowing every inch of his girth. Jameson flinched, stumbling back a bit to rest against the shower wall. He surveyed me, slow, steady, salacious sucks up and down his shaft, in and out of my savory mouth. I welcomed the immense intrusion against my tongue. His groans grew more intense the louder I slurped. And then I felt his hands guiding my head while following my rhythmic flow.

"Gilly, shit, baby. I need to be inside of you."

JD didn't say nothing but a word. My treasure was ready and willing to be crowded by his vast invasion. He effortlessly lifted me as I snaked my legs around his waist. The taste of his member lingered on my tongue as we exchanged dallying, lustful, carnal kisses. Our bodies were confidants, so attuned that his dick stealthily slid into me, requiring no shepherding. His firm hands clutched in mine, my heated flesh affixed to the shower wall. In this precarious position, I couldn't escape the impassioned, unrushed, boundless dips into my pussy. I accommodated every single inch of him.

"Ah, shit. You feel so damn good. You're so fucking deep," I whined, just like he preferred when in this position.

"Man, your ass is spoiled. Shit, Gil," he grunted. "But I love you best, man. Damn."

Caressing and stroking the curves of my face, he willingly swam deeper and deeper into my ocean. Erotic aggression accompanied by loving benevolence was the perfect, intimate combination. After all this time, Jameson's lovemaking still literally snatched my breath away.

Breathless, I whimpered, "I love you more, J."

. . .

I worked out then showered while Gilly was knocked out in my bed. I would never tire of the sight of her butt-ass naked in my bed. With the duvet barely covering her rotund ass, I ogled her—shit, worshiped her pretty ass. The melodious buzz of her faint snore was my meditation. Unbeknownst to Giselle, beholding her was my morning routine. I could sit for hours studying the curves of her face, the fullness of her lips, the steady rise and fall of her chest as she peacefully slumbered. On the mornings when I desired that gorgeous smile, craved her sweet pussy on my tongue, I would giddily disrupt her peace. Today was one of those mornings.

"Gil. Baby. Wake up." I gently trailed a finger down the bridge of her nose. Damn, she was so fucking cute when she pouted.

"No," she whined. "If I wake up, that means you're leaving."

"Two days, Gilly. I'll only be gone for forty-eight hours, baby." I kissed her cheek. She reluctantly sat up, squirming and stretching with that annoying ass squeal.

"You act like you gonna miss a nigga." I nestled into her stomach, trailing tiny kisses up her chest. "Get up, man. I can't miss my flight."

I stared as Giselle ambled her curvy, thick ass body across the room. A fucking marvel.

"Do you think you're ready to go into business with Monroe's?" she mumbled while brushing her teeth.

I was traveling to Detroit to finalize a business deal with the Monroe family. They owned residential and commercial real estate throughout the city of Detroit. Instrumental in rebuilding the inner city, I was ready to expand my reach, and after exhaustive research, a partnership with their company would be a lucrative boss move for me.

"Yeah, that's the plan." I continued to observe her scrambling throughout the room to find her clothes. "Why don't you have more of your shit here? You spend more time here than at your crib."

"Is the Jada Pinkett looking chick going to be there?" Rolling her eyes while ignoring my question, she jumped to fit her plump ass in those damn jeans.

"Yes, she will. You worried about something?" I lifted an angered, yet lustful brow.

"No. Not really."

"Then, nigga, stop talking reckless. Ain't shit on my mind but you." I leered, pissed about this whole exchange.

I grabbed her ass, drawing her near me. Biting the flesh of her exposed stomach, I repeated, "Answer my question, Giselle. Why don't you ever leave your shit here?"

"Your closet and drawers are filled with your shit, J. This is *your* home. No room for little ole me," she bantered.

"I'll make room," I sternly declared.

Gil disjointed from my embrace, avoiding any conversations about us living together. Standing to my full height, I halted her movements. Tenderly cupping her chin, urging her to look at me, I reaffirmed, "Giselle, I will make room for you. Baby, I want you here."

She unhurriedly blinked, remaining hushed, her usual M.O. when we broached the subject. Deciding not to press, I roughly kissed her, stating, "One day soon, your ass won't have a choice."

* * *

Giselle parked the car to drop me off at the airport. It wasn't too busy, so the top-flight security guard didn't hassle us about moving. She rounded the car as I grabbed my bag out of the back seat. I never hesitated to grab her ass, drawing her body into me. Braids in a messy bun, fresh face, and casually dressed in skin-tight jeans and a sweatshirt, she was stunning. We hadn't exchanged many words since we left the house. My intentions were crystal clear, so I didn't desire to bullshit with a whole lotta talking. I wanted Giselle Dean—all day, every day, for the rest of my life.

Gilly snuggled in the folds of my neck, inhaling my scent as I breathed in hers. We kissed and hugged like my ass was going to war.

"Two days," I whispered before biting her ear. "By the time you go to work and play with baby Bellami, I'll be back. Ok?"

She nodded.

"I want to take you somewhere when I get back, so don't make any plans." I nudged her chin then delivered a mouthwatering kiss.

"Ok. Travel safe, bae. I love you more."

Her velvety smooth lips re-connected with mine for the sweetest kiss. I whimpered, "I love you best, baby."

Seventeen

AS I WATCHED Jameson fade into the bustling airport, I drove away at rapid speeds, eager to get to my destination. My road rage was looming because traffic was moving at a snail's pace. I listlessly gazed out of the window, contemplating my impending fate. *I want you here.* Jameson's words played on repeat in my head. *Maybe we're moving too fast? He has so many plans for his future.* The blaring sound throughout the car disrupted my musing.

"Hey, Kay. I'm on my way."

"Ok. Just making sure because I was cooking breakfast. You're still not going to tell me what's going on?" she probed.

"No. This conversation may take all damn day."

Almost thirty minutes later, I lazily strolled into Kayla and Jericho's new home in Grover Heights. The delectable smells of coffee and bacon delighted and disgusted me at the same time.

"Where's my Belly-pop?" I wearily asked, peeking in the bassinet for baby Bellami.

"She's asleep in her room. Eat your food and let's get to talking," Kay instructed.

I followed her to the kitchen table, sadness and anxiety lacing my face.

"Damn, sis, he's only going to be gone for two days. You'll make it—"

Kayla choked on the remaining words when I dumped the contents of the paper bag onto the kitchen island. Three unopened pregnancy tests stared us in the face.

"Oh my God! GG, are you pregnant?" she squealed.

"I don't know, but something feels different. And I have to find out before JD comes back."

Missing my period was not unusual. Since my late teenage years, my menstrual cycle was always unpredictable. Fibroids led to irregular cycles, and crazy cycles turned into endometriosis. While pregnancy wasn't impossible, my doctors made it clear that conception would require more science than art, and a lot of prayers. At thirty-three years old, I'd never had a pregnancy scare like most women my age... until now.

"Different how?" The puzzled, yet excited expression on Kayla's face made me laugh. But just as quickly as the smile came, it vanished.

"I've just been feeling super fat. It could be all of the damn Oreos and jalapeno Cheetos I've been eating. But I'm bloated, nauseous all the time, and I can't fit my bridesmaid's dress for Laiya's wedding." I deliriously sobbed.

"Aww, GG. It's ok, honey. You're not a teenager. You won't get in trouble if you're pregnant." Kay caressed my back.

"It's not that, Kay. Jameson doesn't want a kid right now. He wants to travel the world. Build his empire. Shit, he's in Detroit now, making boss move. A baby fucks up all of his plans," I audibly huffed, slumping into the kitchen chair.

"Well, why don't you take the test first before jumping to

any conclusions. Jameson loves you, GG. He wants what you want. But you gotta be sure first, sweetie."

"You're right," I ceased, reading the test instructions. "It says I have to pee, but I don't have to pee," I whined. I'd lost my mind.

"Bitch, if you don't get in that damn bathroom." Kayla fussed, yanking me from my seat and grabbing the tests on the way to the guest bathroom.

A bottle of water, twenty minutes, and three positive tests later, I was pregnant. Shit, I was stunned, speechless. Kayla lightly tapped on the bathroom door as she opened it. Settled on the floor, I held the tests in my hand, impassively glaring at the word *pregnant.*

"He loves you, Giselle. He *will* want whatever you desire. Do you want this baby, GG?" Kayla whispered, placing the baby monitor on the counter before joining me on the bathroom floor.

I rested my head on her shoulder as my eyes pooled with tears. I sniffed, nodding my head. "Yes. Very much. But I didn't want it like this. I kinda wanted to be somebody's wife before becoming a mother. But yes, I want this baby."

I landed in Detroit and went right into all day meetings. I checked my phone because I hadn't heard from Giselle. I texted her a few times throughout the day and called at least five times since my meetings ended, and her ass hasn't answered.

"This woman stays on some bullshit, man. I bet her damn phone is dead," I whispered to no one but myself as I Face-Timed her again.

Giselle had about another hour to surface before I was getting on a flight back to St. Louis. I contemplated calling

Jericho, but I didn't want to alarm him. Exactly an hour later, my phone rang.

"What the fuck, man. I've been calling you, bae. Are you good?" I fussed at a much higher octave than I intended.

"Yeah. Yes, babe. Sorry, I was with Kay and the baby, and my phone died."

I shook my head.

"I guess Kay's fucking phone died, too, because I called her. Nigga, I was about to call Jericho and get the calvary on your ass," I complained.

"I'm sorry, J. I didn't mean to worry you." Her voice was small, angst.

"Baby, what's going on? What's wrong?"

"Nothing, J. I—I just miss you." She was doing it again, that damn whine.

"I told you I don't want to hear all that whining unless I'm ten strokes deep in you, bae." I chuckled because I thought that shit was funny. But Gilly... not so much.

I believed she missed me because I missed the shit out of her already, but the desolate, despondent tenor of her ordinarily joyful tone was concerning.

"I'm tired, Jameson, and I'm sure you're tired too. You should get some rest—"

The buzz of the FaceTime notification disrupted her attempt to avoid me. I had to see her face. Giselle's expression wrote the story of her mood and would tell me everything I needed to know.

"Look at me, Gilly. No bullshit. Are you ok? You're fucking worrying me, man." I was practically pleading for her to keep it one hundred with me.

"JD, I'm good. Just hurry up and make this move so you can come home," she sullenly muttered.

Gilly blinked those beautiful brown eyes nearly a thousand times as she vainly endeavored to avert her tears. I braced myself because some shit was about to pop off, but I would exonerate her tonight. I audibly sighed, swiping a hand from the top of my head and down my face, distress apparent.

"Ok. Aight, baby. Get some rest," I calmly muttered. But I was far from composed.

She nodded.

"Aye yo," I called, immediately requiring her to maintain eye contact. "I love you more."

Giselle softly smiled. "I love you."

She ended the call.

Wrinkly brow, I eyeballed the phone, baffled, pissed the hell off.

I love you? Gilly and I never settled for just 'I love you', at least not since the night after our fight with Ahmad. *"Loving somebody is easy. I believe Ahmad loved me, but he didn't love me better. Real love should be a constant battle to prove that you love the other person more every day."*

She was slightly tipsy, appropriately fucked, and a bit irrational when she spoke those words that night, resting against my chest, but the shit stuck with me. Since then, it's never been just *I love you* between us because we both toiled daily to manifest the best and more love between us.

That fucking *I love you* bullshit cut like a knife and was a clear indication that something was terribly wrong. I immediately made a phone call.

"Good evening, Mr. Davenport. Is there a problem with your itinerary?" Donna, our family's assistant asked.

"Yes. I need a flight home right away."

* * *

The hour and half flight felt like an eternity. I did leverage the time to send an email to Mr. Monroe and e-sign the documents to officially partner with their company. I arrived in St.

Louis a few minutes after midnight. I usually didn't fuck with the rideshares, but desperate times called for desperate measures. Stepping into the back seat of the black Yukon, I checked my security camera app to determine if Giselle was at my crib or hers. No motion was detected since we left my crib this morning. I requested the driver to change his course and head to Gil's house.

Twenty minutes later, I deactivated her house alarm from my phone before entering the front door. The downstairs was darkened sans the light over the cooktop in the kitchen. Unhurriedly creeping up the steps, I silently prayed that nothing was seriously wrong with Giselle or that she'd changed her mind about loving me... *best*.

Carefully opening the bedroom door, I settled in the threshold regarding her. She was curled in a fetal position, Kindle reader and glasses resting beside her. Just as I'd done almost every morning for the past year, I adoringly surveyed every arc of her pretty face. I rounded the bed, gently perching on the edge. Stroking a finger down the bridge of her nose, I whispered, "baby, I'm home." She lightly tussled at the sensation but drifted back to sleep.

I snickered, trailing my thumb across her lips. "Gilly, baby. Wake up for me, beautiful."

"Mmmh... J, baby," she moaned, rubbing her eyes until the visual of me became clear. "JD! What are you doing here?" Gil awoke.

"You said I love you."

"What?" Her brow creased in confusion.

"You didn't say I love you more or best. Just I love you." I clutched her cheeks in the palm of my hand. "Giselle, talk to me."

"J..." She sighed then swallowed hard, blinking back the mist in her eyes.

"I-you..." Stuttering, she leaned against the headboard,

enfolding her legs into her body. That pretty, pouty face rested on her knees.

"You're making boss moves, J. You are doing everything you said you wanted to do. And I'm just... coasting. Settling for this townhouse, Bonafide has basically stalled, and I just —" She mutedly cried.

"You want what, bae?" I thumbed a single tear away.

"I want more." Giselle shrugged. I'd never seen her this unresolved, insecure.

Peering at her for a long minute, I blurted, "Get up. I want to show you something."

"What? Right now? Jameson, it's late. I'm tired."

"Now, Gil. It won't take long," I promised, kissing against her forehead.

Reluctantly, she dressed in joggers and a hoodie. For some reason, the tears continued to sporadically fall. I didn't fully comprehend what *wanting more* meant for Giselle, but I knew what it meant for me. Besides, I wasn't completely convinced that she was truthfully disclosing her trepidation.

I grabbed her keys and gently nudged her out of the house. Gilly acted like a spoiled brat only when I allowed her to. Usually I would nip this shit in the bud, but I was letting her be a grouch while she processed her apparent unease. We rode in silence, my hand entwined with hers. I parked the car in front of a red two-story brick building in Grover Heights near the new Cartwright Innovation Center.

"JD, are you trying to get us shot?"

"Nah. We're good." I chuckled. "You're always safe with me. Come on."

Giselle remained placid.

"What is this place, Jameson?" Her tone was laced with irritation and her body immobile.

"Nigga, do you trust me?" I yelped, reaching over her to unlatch the seat belt.

She angrily nodded.

I rounded the SUV to retrieve her, clutching her hand, leading her to the double doors. Her brows smacked together when I pulled out a key and opened the door. Gil's furrowed brows slapped into a unibrow when I flicked the light switch, illuminating the space. Bright white walls, with teal and rose gold painted strips provided the backdrop for the *Bonafide Boutique II* glimmering logo on the wall.

Giselle gasped, cupping both hands over her face as she wailed.

"Gil, look at me. Baby, look at me." I smiled, tenderly peeling her fingers from her face. "I was trying to wait until the painting was finished in a couple days, but I see I needed to show you better than I can tell you. Here's your boss move, bae. This is all you. Almost triple the space. Over here, you can sell your oils and shit. And I thought this could be your makeup station." I pointed to the shiny white salon desk. Continuing to give her a tour, I said, "And back there are private rooms for waxing and massages." I searched her saturated orbs for happiness, anger, anything other than tears.

Giselle's beautiful eyes circulated the freshly painted and partially decorated space. Amazement and apprehension dressed her dazzling damp face.

"I wasn't fucking with you when I said I want you, Giselle. I told you once you went down this path, there was no going back. You are mine, baby. We're making these boss moves together. Me and you." I always licked her tears away, metabolizing every particle of her being.

"Talk to me, Gil." I tenderly kissed her lips, softly fluttering against the seam to taste her tongue. "Baby, please."

"Jameson, I—" she croaked, words evaporating in midair.

"Giselle," I breathed out, prepared to risk it all and make her mine.

"I'm pregnant," she muffled.

"Marry me," I stammered.

Our dual confessions harmoniously collided.

Did I hear her correctly? Did my baby say she was having my baby?

"You first." I choked the only words I could unearth.

At this point, Giselle was hysterical. Her cries were so intense she hyperventilated through her confession.

"I didn't think I could get pregnant. You have plans, J, and I'm fucking up everything. You want to travel the world. Build your empire. A baby doesn't fit. I get it. I understand. I didn't mean for this to happen."

Gilly slid down the smooth surface of the receptionist desk, wailing.

I kneeled before her, cupping her chin. "Giselle, baby, breathe." Her shoulders shuddered as she audibly exhaled through puffed cheeks, striving to catch her breath.

"Giselle Dean, I love you more *and* I love you best. You are my everything. My best friend, my homie, my lover, shit, the love of my life." I aggressively gripped her plump cheeks, staring deeply into those reddened eyes.

"Nigga, ain't no fucking empire without you. Boss moves don't mean shit without you, baby. Marry me, Gil. Be my wife. Give me babies." I rested a hand on her flattened stomach, briefly envisioning her exquisite body full with my seed.

"Say yes, Gil. Please say yes," I whispered against her lips, begging.

"Yes. Yes, J. Yes."

I pulled her into my lap as she snuggled into my neck. Her hot tears commingled with mine. I fisted her hair, deeply exhaling the scent of lavender, breathing a sigh of ease and fulfillment.

"It's always been you, Giselle. You are my empire, my dynasty. My most rewarding boss move yet."

THE END... MAYBE

Afterword

Love Note to my Readers

Hey, loves! All I can say is Jameson freaking Davenport! We met Jameson in *Pretty Shattered Soul* and *Pretty Shattered Heart*, but I had no intentions of writing a book about him yet, but he said... I'm ready!

I love his aggressive sexiness and how he loves his best friend, Giselle. That friends to lover entanglement can get a little messy. But in the end, Jameson and Giselle finally realized they were destined to be together.

This won't be the last time you see Jameson and Giselle. The Davenport Family Dynasty is getting a series! Justin, Jeremiah, Jeremi, and Jaxon... who got next?

Follow me on social media to find out! Let me and the world know what you think by leaving a review on Amazon or Goodreads.

The Robbi Renee Collection

- French Kiss Duo

- French Kiss Christmas
- French Kiss New Year
- The Pretty Shattered Series
- Pretty Shattered Soul
- Pretty Shattered Heart
- Pretty Shattered Mind - *Coming Soon*
- Kindred - Xander's Story
- The Love Notes Journal

Join my private Facebook Group - Love Notes.

Follow me on Facebook and Instagram @LoveNotesby-RobbiRenee, on Twitter @LoveRobbi.

www.lovenotesbyrobbirenee.com

Made in the USA
Columbia, SC
30 August 2024

40795051R00085